Unwritten Histories

Unwritten Histories

Craig Cormick

Aboriginal Studies Press 1998

FIRST PUBLISHED IN 1998 BY
　　Aboriginal Studies Press
　　for the Australian Institute of Aboriginal and
　　Torres Strait Islander Studies,
　　GPO Box 553, Canberra ACT 2601

The views expressed in this publication are those of the author and
not necessarily those of the Australian Institute of Aboriginal and
Torres Strait Islander Studies.

The publisher has made every effort to contact copyright owners
for permission to use material reproduced in this book. If your
material has been used inadvertently without permission, please
contact the publisher immediately.

© *CRAIG CORMICK, 1998*
© *JACKIE HUGGINS, 1998* (foreword)
© *GORDON SYRON, 1998* (cover painting)

　　Apart from any fair dealing for the purpose of private study,
　　research, criticism or review, as permitted under the Copyright Act,
　　no part of this publication may be reproduced by any process
　　whatsoever without the written permission of the publisher.

*NATIONAL LIBRARY OF AUSTRALIA CATALOGUING-IN-
PUBLICATION DATA:*

　　Cormick, Craig.
　　Unwritten histories.

　　ISBN 0 85575 316 1.

　　1. Aborigines, Australian — History. 2. Aborigines,
　　Australian — Social life and customs. I. Title.

　　994.0049915

COVER: Gordon Syron, *Land Rights — Sydney, 1788*, 1998,
　　oil on oil-based paper, 26 x 20.5 cm
　　(photograph by Elaine Pelot Kitchener)
EDITED BY Stephanie Haygarth, Canberra
DESIGNED AND TYPESET BY Brown & Co Typesetters, Canberra
PRINTED IN AUSTRALIA BY Griffin Press Pty Ltd, Adelaide

'If Australia is to be changed ... then the kinds of stories we tell about Australia will have to change.'

Stephen Muecke, *No Road*, 1997.

'The barriers which for so long kept Aboriginal experience out of our history books were not principally those of source material or methodology but rather ones of perception and preference.'

Henry Reynolds, *The Other Side of the Frontier*, 1981.

Contents

Foreword	ix
Acknowledgements	xiii
Author's notes	xv
Terra Nullius — the Unknown Country	1
Buckley's Chance	15
Charles Darwin Views the Future	23
The Last History of Jorgen Jorgensen	31
Sorry Business	39
The Unknown South Land	51
Do You Remember When You Heard Kennedy Had Been Killed?	65
The Three Gospels of the Reverend Lancelot Threlkeld	75
Dig: The Forgotten History of Burke and Wills	87
The Event of the Century	101
Ned Kelly Dreaming	109
Mrs Watson Escapes the Cannibals	117
Krao — the Missing Link	127
Jandamarrajandamarrajandamarra!	137
The Last Battle	151
Mrs Shackleton's Freezer	159
Pastor Strehlow's Journey to the Land of Death	169
Lasseter's Last Dream	179
Bibliography	185

Foreword

Until recently Aboriginal people were denied a place in Australian history. The devastating introduction of European diseases; the land expropriation; the massacres; the efforts of churches, governments and pastoral interests to decimate traditional Aboriginal cultures; the forced removal of children; our labour history; and the exploitation of Aboriginal women as sexual chattels and slaves were never recorded in the history texts.

Accordingly Aboriginal people were never considered, in history, to have had any influence or impact on the economy of national development. Aboriginal guides (as evidenced by Truganini), steeped in local knowledge and bush skills, paved the way for many explorers. In the cattle industry, Aboriginal men and women worked as stockmen and women and as domestic servants. This book unravels many of these unwritten histories, so that Aboriginal economic, cultural, political and intellectual spheres are not peripheral, but central to the story.

This is where Australian history begins: not some 210 years ago when the white man set foot on this continent's soil, but at the beginning when there was a nation of Indigenous peoples sustaining and nurturing the environment for many thousands of years. The inclusion of their presence is vital to the understanding of the whole picture.

Ironically, *Unwritten Histories* is based on the premise — which has been held for too long — that history only begins from when it is written, and Australia's history has mostly been written from the British colonisers' point of view.

As there are different experiences of the world and different bases of experience, so too there are different versions of history: it is simplistic to think that there is only one. An account of an event may vary considerably according to the observer's background, race, ethnicity, age, gender, education, vested interests, empathy, bias or whether they are the victor or the loser in any situation. One must be aware, though, that when 'history' is recorded from one of these positions, a version is constructed that may in turn be imposed upon those whose lives it touches, as their retrospective reality. Therefore interpretations of history differ according to cultural perspectives and also perspectives of time.

Historians and creative writers both seek to find the truth about characters and their interplay with each other and their environments, and to interpret the patterns of thought that define their actions. But while historians are often limited to interpreting existing written records, a creative writer is more able to ask 'What if … ?' and seek to express other truths beyond those that are known.

These stories are fiction, but they are based very closely on well-researched facts, and reveal many truths about Australia's 'unwritten history' to us. Craig Cormick quite successfully finds a way to explain diverse positions in a convincing atmosphere that introduces past and present reactions. He explicitly reveals how the present, and a reformist political agenda in particular, shape his perspectives.

There is always more than one history, and rarely one 'true' history. The stories in this book show that there is a lot more to history than how it is recorded, and also that Australia's Indigenous peoples have a long history (often recorded orally) that has been too long 'unwritten' or overlooked and marginalised.

In order to write about Aborigines and Europeans, an examination of their relations with one another over time is necessary. Their relationships to each other are often couched in terms of power and conflict. There are too few examples of mutual friendships and understanding allowed to foster during the traumatic frontier times.

FOREWORD

Unwritten Histories is what Indigenous people would term a 'deadly' book, so expressing their delight in seeing how understandings and presentations of the past of Indigenous and non-Indigenous people are being creatively re-enacted. This book is obviously a text that needs to be read as widely as possible throughout schools and the community.

Jackie Huggins
Aboriginal and Torres Strait Islander Unit
University of Queensland

Acknowledgements

Many of the stories in this collection were worked on or worked out during a Varuna Mentorship Program in early 1998. Thanks to Inez Baranay for her skilled mentoring and to Cathy Cole, Lyn Tawa and Madeline Byrne for their constructive criticisms.

Also thanks to Steve Evans at the University of Canberra's Centre for Writing and Cultural Studies for his input to many of these stories.

And a special thanks to Cate Kennedy, a good friend and a great critic, and to Stephanie Haygarth, a first-rate editor.

I am indebted to the ACT Library Service and the National Library of Australia for their wonderful collections of historical material.

Finally, this collection is dedicated to all those men and women who have been 'unwritten' throughout Australia's history.

Author's notes

The following stories have been previously published in full or condensed forms:

Lasseter's Last Dream in *Blast #33*, 1997; Terra Nullius — the Unknown Country in the *Canberra Times*, 31 January 1998; Mrs Shackleton's Freezer in the *Canberra Times*, 28 February 1998; Do You Remember When You Heard Kennedy Had Been Killed? in the *Canberra Times*, 14 March 1998, and *Green Left Weekly*, 18 March 1998; and The Last Battle, in *Green Left Weekly*, 22 April 1998.

The Three Gospels of the Reverend Lancelot Threlkeld was highly commended in the 1997 Judah Waten National Story Writing Competition, Ned Kelly Dreaming won a special mention in the 1997 R Carson Gold Short Story Competition, and The Unknown South Land won second prize in the 1998 R Carson Gold Short Story Competition.

There are many different spellings for the name of 'Truganini', and in the story Sorry Business the spelling 'Trugernanna' is used, as it was the spelling used by George Augustus Robinson in his journals.

The passages of speech in the story Pastor Strehlow's Journey to the Land of Death are taken directly from *Journey to Horse Shoe Bend*, by his son, TGH Strehlow (1969). The structure of this story is based on Aranda creation stories and the dialogue stanzas are based on Aranda traditional songs.

All the stories in *Unwritten Histories* are based on historical characters or events. Throughout the book, material taken from original sources is quoted in italics, unless otherwise indicated, and full details of these sources may be found in the bibliography.

Terra Nullius — the Unknown Country

Eastern Australia, 1770

'The ocean is eternal,' says Banks, and wrings his hands. 'Does it never end?'

Cook points his telescope to the horizon and says, 'Of course it ends.' He finds Banks' rhetorical flourishes rather absurd at times.

Cook and Banks stand by the rail of HM bark *Endeavour*, peering at the western horizon. They have been nineteen days at sea since leaving New Zealand. If the great southern land truly exists, they should sight it any day now.

'I've been thinking,' says Banks.

'That's rare,' mumbles Cook.

'Yes, about Dalrymple's theory of the great southern land.'

'Indeed!' says Cook, who thinks that Dalrymple and his theories are also absurd.

'Yes,' says Banks. 'He argues well that the southern hemisphere should contain a land mass of equal size to the northern hemisphere, to properly balance the globe, but if the southern continent were mostly mountainous, it could therefore be smaller in land size, could it not?'

'Or,' says Cook, 'you could argue that the oceans in the southern seas might simply be shallower.'

Banks thinks on that for a moment. Then looks over the rail for land. There is none.

'What do you think the great southern land might be like?' he asks.

'All unknown countries are the same in one manner,' says Cook, his eye still at the telescope. He feels they must reach land soon, and he is keen to sight it first.

'And what manner is that?' enquires Banks.

'They are all unknowable until you have reached them.'

Banks muses. 'Did you know that Shakespeare called the future the unknown country?' he asks.

'Did he indeed?' says Cook, who as the son of a Yorkshire farmer once dreamed of the sea, an unknown entity, years before he ever saw it. 'Well we've not yet sailed there either, although I dare say we might,' he says.

'Do you know what I miss most?' asks Banks.

'What is that?' asks Cook, without looking around.

'Tahiti,' says Banks. He says it like a warm breeze. 'It comes back to me in my dreams.'

Cook, the elder of the two men by 14 years, says nothing. He knows Banks is thinking of the half-naked, brown-skinned Tahitian girls. Breasts like small melons. Large smiles upon their faces. Walking along the waterline of the beach, dragging their toes in the warm ocean's spume.

'Ah well,' says Banks. 'I think I'll go down below for a bit.'

Cook turns to watch him go.

'Land ahoy!' shouts a lieutenant up in the rigging.

The crew rush up on deck, overjoyed to see land again, and that afternoon Cook writes in his journal:

> *The Southernmost point of land we had in sight, which bore from us W $^1/_4$ S, I judged to lay in the Latitude of 38° 0' S and in the Long of 211° 7' W from the Meridian of Greenwich. I have named it Point Hicks, because Lieutenant Hicks was the first who discover'd this Land. To the Southward of this point we could see no land and yet it was clear in that Quarter, and by our Longitude compared with that of Tasman's, the body of Van Diemen's land ought to have bore due S from us, and from the soon falling of the Sea after the wind abated I had reason to think it did; but*

as we did not see it, and finding the Coast to trend NE and SW, or rather more to the Westward, makes me Doubtfull whether they are one land or no.

The *Endeavour* bark sails up the eastern coast of this unknown country, as Cook names the bays and inlets, looking for a safe place to land. The crew hang off the rigging expectantly, looking for any resemblance to Tahiti in the shape of the beaches they pass.

On Saturday 28 April they reach a large open bay and spy the smoke of several fires. The following day their ship enters the bay majestically and they see several natives on the shore who do not even appear to notice them.

A longboat is readied and sent ashore. Young Isaac Smith, Cook's wife's own cousin, is granted the honour of being the first to set foot on this new land.

Saw, as we came in, on both points of the bay, several of the Natives and a few hutts; Men, Women, and Children on the S Shore abreast of the Ship, to which place I went in the Boats in hopes of speaking with them, accompanied by Mr Banks, Dr Solander, and Tupia. As we approached the Shore they all made off, except 2 Men, who seem'd resolved to oppose our landing. As soon as I saw this I order'd the boats to lay upon their Oars, in order to speak to them; but this was to little purpose, for neither us nor Tupia could understand one word they said. We then threw some nails, beads, etc, ashore, which they took up, and seem'd not ill pleased with, in so much that I thought that they beckon'd to us to come ashore; but in this we were mistaken, for as soon as we put the boat in they again came to oppose us, upon which I fir'd a musqet between the 2, which had no other Effect than to make them retire back, where bundles of their darts lay, and one of them took up a stone and threw at us, which caused my firing a Second Musquet, load with small Shott; and altho' some of the shott struck the man, yet it had no other effect than making him lay hold on a Target. Immediately after this we landed, which we had no sooner done than they throw'd 2 darts at us; this obliged me to fire a third shott, soon after which they both made off, but not in such haste but what we might have taken one; but Mr Banks being of Opinion that the darts were poisoned, made me cautious how I advanced into the Woods.

The beach of this land impresses the crew greatly. It is fine white sand. They walk up and down its length endlessly. Or they stand on the shore and catch fish from the sea.

'It is good to be on solid land again,' says Banks. And he persuades Cook to take to walking the sands.

The first sight of the white skin of the naked crewmen, as they swim in the ocean, shocks Cook. He realises that it has indeed been a long time since they left the warm climes of Tahiti to roam the chill southern oceans.

Some of the men play in the waters. Some search for crabs amongst the rocks. One of the marines is using the sand to build a model of a fortress.

Cook watches some of the sailors hauling in a fishing net. It has many stingrays in it and he decides to call this Stingray Bay.

Then Joseph Banks approaches him. His arms are full of plants. He praises the abundance of undiscovered flora in this new land, and then asks Cook if he would command some of the men to help him find his keys to his botany chest, as he has lost them in the sand.

The men kick around futilely in the sand until it is dark and Cook decides instead to name this place Botany Bay.

Thursday, 3rd May — Winds at SE, a Gentle breeze and fair weather. In the PM I made a little excursion along the Sea Coast to the Southward, accompanied by Mr Banks and Dr Solander. At our first entering the woods we saw 3 of the

Natives, who made off as soon as they saw us; more of them were seen by others of our people, who likewise made off as soon as they found they were discover'd. In the AM I went in the Pinnace to the head of the bay, accompanied by Drs Solander and Monkhouse, in order to Examine the Country, and to try to form some Connections with the Natives ... After we had sufficiently examin'd this part we return'd to the Boat, and seeing some Smoke and Canoes and 6 small fires near the Shore, and Muscles roasting upon them, and few Oysters laying near; from this we conjectured that there had been just 6 people, who had been out each in his Canoe picking up the Shell fish, and come to a Shore to eat them, where each had made his fire to dress them by. We tasted of their Cheer, and left them in return Strings of beads, etc. The day being now far spent, we set out on our return to the Ship.

Cook is strolling along the beach alone and suddenly feels an urgent need to pass a stool. It must be the large bird they cooked for dinner last night, he thinks. As large as an ostrich, but as tough as a marine's boots. The pressure squeezes against his stomach.

He looks around him and decides to walk into the trees a little. He climbs the dunes, his shoes sinking into the soft sand, until he reaches the trees. Out of sight, he unfastens his breeches and squats down, loosening his bowels.

One huge push and out it comes, a great soft stool. The relief in his gut is immediate. He looks back at it. It seems more yellow than normal, and full of sand.

But the flies are upon the stool almost immediately. Cook looks around for some soft leaves to clean his posterior. But the trees nearby are bent and gnarled with spiky leaves. He considers them a moment and then breaks off a handful.

They are even worse than they look. Prickly and painful. Like Banks, he thinks. And he decides to name this tree a Banksia.

> *Sunday, 6th May — The natives do not appear to be numerous, neither do they seem to live in large bodies, but dispers'd in small parties along by the Water side. Those I saw were about as tall as Europeans, of a very dark brown Colour, but not black, nor had they woolly frizled hair, but black and lank like ours. No sort of Cloathing or Ornaments were ever seen by any of us upon any one of them, or in or about any of their Hutts; from which I conclude that they never wear any. Some that we saw had their faces and bodies painted with a sort of White Paint or Pigment.*

Cook looks up and sees three of the sailors walking along the beach towards him. They are wearing a thick cream on their noses and upper cheeks. Most bizarre, thinks Cook.

He stops the men and questions them. He asks them if they have painted their faces in some imitation of the markings used by the natives. But they tell him, no, this is a paste to prevent sunburn, prescribed by Mr Banks.

Cook shakes his head a little. A passing fancy that will never last, he thinks.

Cook sits with his journal and tries to describe this fine beach at Botany Bay that they have found, so that others may know it as they have known it.

> *Sunday, 6th May — It is situated in the Lat of 34° 0' S, Long 208° 37' W. It is capacious, safe, and Commodious; it may be known by the land on the Sea Coast, which is of a pretty even and moderate height, Rather higher than it is inland, with steep rocky Clifts next the Sea, and looks like a long Island lying close under the Shore. The Entrance of the Bay lies about the Middle of this land. In coming from the Southward it is discover'd before you are abreast of it, which you cannot do in coming from the Northward; the entrance is little more than a Quarter of a Mile broad, and*

lies in WNW. To sail into it keep the S shore on board until within a small bare Island, which lies close under the North Shore.

Cook leads a small expedition up the beach. They cross a few dunes and suddenly there is a thick forest before them. The trees seem to grow out of the sand and the grass is coarse and prickly.

The trees and bushes pluck at Cook and his men as they make their way into the forest. Insects swarm out of dark, cool places and assault them.

The harsh light makes the darkness of the shade seem alive, as if there are snakes and hostile natives lurking there.

'Keep your eyes out for natives,' says Cook, glancing around.

He turns and sees that they can no longer see the beach. No longer see the ocean. Two years at sea and never once out of sight of the ocean. Cook suddenly feels very giddy. His legs start to wobble, pitching slightly under him. He holds out his arms for balance and feels the bushland closing in on him. The trees are waving spears and clubs at him. The bracken on the ground slithers menacingly close.

Cook turns to the lieutenant beside him and says, 'I think we should return now!' and starts fighting his way back through the vegetation.

'Excuse me sir,' says the lieutenant, pointing in another direction. 'It is this way back to the beach.'

Cook turns and silently leads the way through the trees, which are motionless as he passes.

Sunday, 6th May — During our stay in this Harbour I caused the English Colours to be display'd ashore every day, and an inscription to be cut out upon one of the Trees near the Watering place, setting forth the Ship's Name, Date, etc. Having seen everything this place afforded, we, at daylight in the morning, weigh'd with a light breeze at NW, and put to Sea, and the wind soon after coming to the Southward we steer'd along shore NNE, and at Noon we

> *were by observation in the Latitude of 33° 50' S, about 2 or 3 Miles from the Land, and abreast of a Bay, wherein there appear'd to be safe Anchorage, which I called Port Jackson.*

Cook sails northwards and maps the land, naming every mountain, bay and inlet. But he misses the mouth of the Hunter River and the Brisbane River.

They put ashore on the sandy beach of an inlet that Cook has decided to name Thirsty Sound. They have been unable to find any water there. It is a fine beach though. The day is warm and the breakers roll lazily onto the sand.

Banks, standing beside Cook, regards the sunshine and the surf and suddenly says, 'Do you know, I have a sudden craving for an ale, and also for some iced cream. What do you make of that?'

'Absurd,' says Cook, clapping both hands behind his back. But he can feel the craving in his mouth too.

Navigating the reefs they have encountered is tedious and careful work. They can't afford to make an error and end up on the sharp coral below them.

Banks says, 'It's like a whole mountainous land in shallow water, just under the ship.'

Cook, lying in his bunk at nights, feels its sharpness near the timbers of his ship. And, drifting off to sleep, he dreams of having a glass panel in his ship through which he can view the coral as they sail past it.

And he wakes with an odd memory that this dream was like one he had many years before, as a young boy, before he ever saw the sea. A dream of water stretching beyond sight. Stretching beyond the future.

Monday, 11 June. Disaster. The *Endeavour* bark strikes a submerged reef.

TERRA NULLIUS — THE UNKNOWN COUNTRY

Before 10 o'Clock we had 20 and 21 fathoms, and Continued in that depth until a few minutes before 11, when we had 17, and before the Man and the Lead could have another cast, the Ship Struck and stuck fast. Immediately upon this we took in all our Sails, hoisted out the Boats and Sounded round the Ship, and found that we had got upon the SE Edge of a reef of Coral Rocks, having in some places round the Ship 3 and 4 fathoms Water, and in other places not quite as many feet, and about a Ship's length from us on the starboard side (the Ship laying with her Head to the NE) were 8, 10, and 12 fathoms. As soon as the Long boat was out we struck Yards and Topmast, and carried out the Stream Anchor on our Starboard bow, got the Coasting Anchor and Cable into the Boat, and were going to carry it out in the same way; but upon my sounding the 2nd time round the Ship I found the most waters a Stern, and therefore had this Anchor carried out upon the Starboard Quarter, and hove upon it a very great Strain; which was to no purpose, the Ship being quite fast, upon which we went to work to lighten her as fast as possible, which seem'd to be the only means we had left to get her off.

It takes a week to get the ship ashore so that the carpenters can begin repairing the damage. Cook oversees the repairs, impatient at the slow progress. It seems harder to rally the crew to work each day. They appear more intent on sleeping in the shade and drinking out of coconut shells. Sometimes they rally themselves for a game of cricket on the sand.

The weather is very hot and Cook sweats heavily in his full naval jacket and stockings.

The sailors have taken to wearing cut-down shirts and breeches, and also to painting ridiculous slogans on their shirts.

Mr Banks presents Cook with a cut-down shirt for his own use. The slogan daubed on it says 'COOK RULES OK'.

Cook has to ask Banks to explain it to him. Several times.

Some men are walking on the beach, examining the flotsam and jetsam at the high tide mark, mostly seaweed and small marine creatures. Suddenly one of the men yelps and hops to one foot, as if he has been bitten. His companions inspect the wound to his foot and see that he has trodden on some broken glass. Thrown overboard from their own ship.

Cook wonders whether to write up in his log the fact that the men are playing a new game on the beach. It involves rigging up a high net and hitting a ball back and forward over it. He thinks he will steal a glimpse into Banks's journal later and see what words he has used to describe it. He wishes that words would come to him as easily as they did to Banks. He also wishes that the men would work more on repairing the ship — but he can't help wondering what the feel of slapping the ball over the net would be like.

> *Thursday, 28th June — Fresh breezes and Cloudy. All hands employ'd as Yesterday.*

After six weeks the crew have come to regard this stretch of sand and water as their own. Already the men are jokingly calling their little tent village 'Cooktown'.

On some mornings Cook himself imagines a long line of houses leading back from the dunes.

All the banksias would be cut down, he thinks, and replaced with palms or perhaps English trees. Oaks and maples, perhaps. He imagines his own small stone cottage sitting there at the end of the beach. His wife waiting for him within.

And suddenly another image springs into Cook's mind. Half-naked, brown-skinned Tahitian girls. Breasts like small melons. Large smiles upon their faces. Walking along the waterline of the beach, dragging their toes in the warm ocean's spume.

He wants to lie down on the warm sand and watch a procession of half-naked tanned young girls, all day long. Every day.

He closes his eyes and lets the thought wash over him like a cool breeze.

'Captain. Captain!' The urgency of the shout rouses him and he opens his eyes. There is a small band of blacks advancing upon them down the beach. They have come out of the bushes. They had been hiding in the shadows there. Who knows how long they had been there watching them?

One of the marines runs to the camp for his musket. Two of the other marines pick up large sticks, like spears, and wave them menacingly at the natives. But they do not retreat.

Cook watches and then asks the men to lower their weapons. With a hastily summoned armed escort, he goes to meet the natives. He walks with his hands grasped tightly behind his back. He watches them carefully as they approach. And suddenly he resents their presence. He resents their intrusion into his daydream. He resents their trespassing upon his beach. And he resents the fact that they are not Tahitian maidens.

They will be ready to leave in a day or two. Cook will issue the order to sail, but he wants a part of him to stay here as well. That night he writes in his journal:

> *About this time 5 of the Natives came over and stay'd with us all the Forenoon. There were 7 in all — 5 Men, 1 Woman, and a Boy; these 2 last stay'd on the point of Land on the other side of the River about 200 Yards from us. We could very clearly see with our Glasses that the Woman was as naked as ever she was born; even those parts which I always before now thought Nature would have taught a woman to Conceal were uncovered.*

Banks stands on the white sands with Cook, watching the sunset. They have traded beads with the natives and learned some of the New Holland language. Cook has written some of the words in his journal: the head is *whageegee*, the penis is *keveil*, the sun is *galan*, the sky is *kere* and a canoe is *maragan*.

'I wonder what they will tell of us?' Banks asks. 'What will they make of our coming and departure?'

'When we have gone it might all seem a dream to them,' says Cook.

'Perhaps,' says Banks. 'But a dream of what?'

On Saturday 4 August the *Endeavour* bark is at sea again.

Cook sits in his cabin working on one of his many fine charts. He takes great pride in them.

Banks is watching his slow meticulous work.

'Imagine it,' says Banks, 'Over two thousand miles of beaches.'

'But how do I describe it to the Home Office?' asks Cook. He stands and places his hands behind his back. He does not want Banks to see he is wringing them. 'I can say how many ships could safely anchor in each harbour we have charted. I can describe the tall pines as suitable for ships' masts. But how do I describe the beaches? Are they exploitable materials?'

'But their richness is beyond commercial value,' argues Banks.

Cook thinks on this for a moment. 'I will describe this land as uninhabited. *Terra nullius*.'

'But what about the natives?' asks Banks.

'They live in the forests,' says Cook. 'I'm referring to the beaches.'

Wednesday, 22nd August — Gentle breezes at E by S and clear weather ... Having satisfied myself of the great probability of a passage, thro' which I intend going with the Ship, and therefore may land no more upon this Eastern coast of New Holland, and on the Western side I can make no new discovery, the honour of which belongs to the Dutch Navigators, but the Eastern Coast from the Lat of 38° S down to this place, I am confident, was never seen or Visited by any European before us; and notwithstanding I had in the Name of his Majesty taken possession of several places upon this Coast, I now once More hoisted English Colours, and in the Name of His Majesty King George the Third took possession of the whole Eastern coast from the above Lat down to this place by the Name of New Wales, together with all the Bays, Harbours, Rivers, and the Islands, situated upon the said Coast; after which we fired 3 Volleys of small Arms, which were answer'd by the like number from the Ship.

Then Cook sails northwards. Towards known lands. Towards home. Leaving the unknown land of the future now behind him.

Buckley's Chance

Port Phillip, 1835

William Buckley stands between the natives and the settlers, with the sound of approaching death in his ears. It is like light footsteps rapidly advancing through the shadows about him. He knows it is very, very close. But he does not know how to face it or deflect it. He closes his eyes as the two peoples fling harsh whispered words at him. 'What are the natives muttering, Buckley?' his countrymen ask him. 'Why are the white men uneasy, Murrangurk?' his tribesmen demand.

He has the words in his mouth to tell them. In both languages. But he cannot say them. He opens his eyes again. He stands head and shoulders above the tallest black or white man gathered around him, but still he wishes he were taller. Wishes he could stretch his long limbs wide enough to embrace the two cultures.

The tribespeople and the settlers tug at him. Pulling him back to each of them. Back to where they want him to belong.

'Tell us,' they urge. 'Tell us!' But the words have stuck inside him. In both tongues. He feels himself being torn in two. Feels the strain right through his huge chest, opening up a cavity within him. Feels the words dropping down into it.

And then a young settler boy, who has been friendly with the natives, steps forward. 'The natives are planning to massacre us,' he whispers. Death is all around. People move quickly. Grasping muskets. Fingering clubs. Cocking guns. Staring tensely.

Now that it has been said, the moment of danger passes. William Buckley hears the faint footsteps of death receding from him.

Then the blacks are stepping away. Lowering spears.

But both his peoples now stare at him. Spit out his names. 'Buckley!' 'Murrangurk!' He has betrayed them. He closes his eyes again and wishes he could relive the moment. Wishes he could make it turn out differently.

Only ten days after slipping away from the settlement at Sullivans Bay, William Buckley was alone and quite lost. He had made his slow way around the large bay in the company of his fellow absconders. But their fears and hunger got the better of them. Fearful of the unknown land about them they had turned back, eager to return to the harsh convict life they had been so quick to flee. Defeated, they bade William Buckley farewell and set out on the long walk back to the violence and oppression of the doomed settlement. They were never seen again.

William Buckley kept his eyes on that far-off settlement and the ship *Calcutta*, as he made his way around the bay. He felt that if he kept travelling around the shore he would eventually come full circle and end up back at the settlement again. So he took to the bush to the west. Where he hoped Sydney might lie.

He was quickly surrounded by strange plants and animals that he could not even name. But he kept walking. He was 23 years old, young, strong. A former soldier. Had marched into and out of many battles. He was tall as a mountain and trusted the strength in his large body. He was confident that he would survive in this strange land.

William Buckley is on the brink of despair. His steps are faltering. He is starving. He cannot catch the small animals that scream and taunt him in the night. The few plants he nibbles on are bitter; water is scarce. He finds some shellfish and berries and tries to conserve his great strength. He must keep walking if he is to survive.

There are natives in the woods. He spies the smoke from their fires and sometimes sees them at a distance. He has heard stories that they are cannibals. He hides from them. Fear grows inside him with the growing hunger and weakness.

He no longer knows the way back towards the settlement. Doubts he has the strength to make it even if he were to turn back. He keeps walking slowly onwards. Not knowing how he might survive in this strange land.

In the afternoon he comes across a grave. A broken spear protruding from the mound of earth sends a long shadow towards him. He places one foot on the grave, and wrestles the spear free. It will serve him for a walking stick, he thinks. To support his weight.

He walks onwards. Towards the native camp.

The first word the blacks teach him is *Murrangurk*. His new name. For one who has been reborn from the land of death.

The men and women recognise the spear he last carried when he was killed in battle. They quickly surround him, appearing from the shadows, attacking him with strange words. Curious to know how he has journeyed back from the land of the dead. Observing that the journey has altered his skin and voice. Robbed him of his knowledge and language.

'Murrangurk,' the Wothuwurong people say, over and over, encouraging him to say it.

'Murrangurk,' he says. They smile. He is reborn amongst them.

They teach him how to speak again. Slow word by word. They feed him, coaxing the unfamiliar food into his mouth. Coaxing the strange words out.

Bemin the possum. *Karwer* the emu. *Ko-im* the kangaroo. *Wimba* the wallaby.

As he re-learns their words, they tell him his story. How he first came to live with them. They talk of the Kulin tribes that live across the land and show him his totem — the magpie. They recount his deeds and battles. Remind him how he died in battle. And then how he journeyed back from the land of the dead to return to them. Came full circle.

Murrangurk lies alone in his shelter some nights, unsure if he is dreaming or awake. He listens for the sound of the *ngarangs* and other deadly spirits prowling in the dark. Some nights he can hear the approach of death in his ears. He covers them to block it out.

In battle he has seen the bravest warriors taunt their enemies into hurling their sharp, barbed spears at them. Facing death as it rapidly flies towards them. Listening for its approach. Then they quickly sidestep death, or hold up a small shield and knock it aside.

But he can never move so quickly. Knows he is spared from battle as one who has already died, but he fears death when it is close to him. Is shaken by the savage randomness of it. Some nights he can still hear the thud of the spear striking his adopted son. Can still hear the victorious shout of the Collenbitchik tribe as he falls to the ground.

Death seems always so close about him. The thud of the spear. The hard crack of the war club. The thwack of the axe. He cannot block out the sounds. They are as constant as the threat of attack from the hostile tribes of the Jajowurong, the Warengbadawa and the Pallidurgbarran.

He knows that other members of the tribe do not return from the land of death.

Murrangurk approaches the white men's camp hesitantly. He can see tents. Their boats are drawn up on the shore. He has walked right back around the bay to where the white men have returned. He feels he has come full circle. He can count three white men and six strange blacks.

They all look up and stare in surprise. He has appeared amongst them like a ghost. As tall as a forest giant. Long hair and beard down to his waist. Spears held tightly in his hand.

They make signs of peace, urge him to sit down amongst them. They try to talk to him. He can understand their words, but cannot find the words in him to reply.

Then one hands him some food. Says the word to him, 'Bread!' He places the soft substance into his mouth. And he knows the food. The memory of it is somewhere distant within him. He feels it melting in his mouth. Melting his stiff tongue. 'Bread,' he says.

The white men look at him carefully. Trying to make out what kind of a native this giant man is. He tries to say his name. But those words won't come easily. He shows them the tattoo on his arm, with the letters WB and slowly the words emerge. 'William,' he says. 'William Buckley.'

The white men stare in amazement as they help him coax the words out. First a trickle. Then a hesitant flow. He tells them his story. He is the sole survivor of a shipwreck, he says. The lies come so easy in English. He has lived with the blacks as a member of their tribe. He has not seen a white man for perhaps some 20 years.

And then the men tell him the year. It is 1835. He counts the years — and keeps counting. Thirty-two years have passed since he was last William Buckley!

New people arrive each month. Ships sail into the bay and unload settlers and supplies and animals. Sheep are soon as numerous across the land as the plague scabs had been across the bodies of the Kulin people some seasons previously. They had called them *Lillipook Mindie* — scales of the ancient serpent — and they had brought death and devastation.

Now a new plague of settlers and their livestock spreads across the land, driving away the animals. *Bemin* the possum. *Karwer* the emu. *Ko-im* the kangaroo. *Wimba* the wallaby.

The settlers trade axes and cloth for the Kulin people's land. They run their sheep upon it. Fell the trees. Plant crops. Chase the natives away with guns when they return.

William Buckley, newly employed as Superintendent of Natives for the colony, tells his stories of the white men to his tribespeople. Tells his story of the natives to the settlers. Tries to bring his two peoples closer together. Tries to keep them further apart. Tries to explain to each that they have little real understanding of the other. Tries to tell them his real story. But the words won't come to him.

He listens to the settlers as they tell him how he should negotiate with the natives for them. He listens to his tribespeople as they tell him how he can take up their grievances with the settlers. Some days he is William Buckley, shipwreck survivor. Some days he is Murrangurk, reborn from the dead. Some days he no longer sure who he is.

He lies alone in his new cottage at night. Listens for the sound of death approaching. Hears it in the discharge of muskets. The dull thud of spears. The sharpening of long knives. The hard crack of the war club. The lusty breath that accompanies venereal disease. The ringing clink of spirit bottles. The hacking cough of deep lung infections. Hears it all around him. No longer random, its inevitability is what he fears. He covers his ears to block it out.

William Buckley stands between the natives and the settlers. Turns around as his peoples call his name and stare at him. Goes full circle. 'Buckley!' they hiss. 'Murrangurk!' they spit. He has betrayed them.

A young settler boy, who has been friendly with the natives, has stepped forward and hissed the words he could not say, 'The natives are planning to massacre the settlers!'

Death is all around. People move quickly. Grasping muskets. Fingering clubs. Cocking guns. Staring tensely. Facing each other bravely. Now that it is said, the moment of danger passes. The natives step away. Lowering spears. He hears death receding. It has been deflected once more.

The tribespeople and the settlers step away from him. No longer tugging at him. No longer each pulling him back to them. No longer willing to listen to his stories.

'What are the natives muttering, Buckley?' his countrymen had asked. 'Why are the white men uneasy, Murrangurk?' his tribesmen had demanded.

'Tell us,' they had urged. 'Tell us!' But the words had stuck inside him. In two tongues. He felt himself being torn in two. Felt the strain right through his huge chest. He felt a cavity opening up within him and felt the words dropping down into it.

He closes his eyes and wishes he could relive the moment. Wishes he could make it turn out otherwise. But he knows that there is no other way of deflecting death. He opens his eyes again. He stands head and shoulders above the tallest black or white man gathered around him. But still he wishes he were taller. Knows he will never be able to stretch his long limbs wide enough to bridge his two cultures.

Charles Darwin Views the Future

The Blue Mountains, 1836

Charles Darwin is standing on the very edge of the abyss. Can feel it drawing him forward. He leans a little further out, tries to see how far it plummets below. Tries to peer through the mist and the low clouds obscuring his vision. Tries to see right to the bottom. Then a sudden sense of giddiness assails him. Grasps him tightly and pulls him beyond the very edge. Then over. He feels himself falling.

'Steady Mr Darwin,' says his guide, grabbing his arm. 'These cliffs are over a 100 yards high. If you fall from here you'll be lost to science forever.'

Charles Darwin nods his head a little. Clears it. Steps back from the edge. Then he says, 'The escarpment is everything you promised. Quite spectacular.'

He turns and looks away from the pull of the cliff, towards the large jagged rock formations the guide had indicated earlier. 'What did you say the three rock formations were called?' he asks.

'They are the Three Sisters,' says the guide.

For the past four years Charles Darwin has been exploring the jungles and land formations of South America. He has climbed the Andes Mountains and walked the dry pampas plains. Has camped overnight in the jungles and has been bitten by almost every flea and mite that inhabits the cheap hotels of that continent. But he has amassed an unsurpassed collection of natural science: fossils, plants, rocks, skeletons and living animals.

He has discovered many new species, and he has discovered many things he cannot as yet describe. He found sea shells in a long, thin strata line in a cliff face, hundreds of feet above the sea. He found fossil remains of extinct animals, like the enormous *Toxidon*, which was exact in every way but scale to living capybaras. And he found finches on the Galapagos Islands where, on each island, the birds had a different-shaped beak.

During the long sea voyages of the HMS *Beagle*, he fingers the bones he has collected and goes over his notes and thinks about these things. As if they are parts of some obscure jigsaw puzzle that he is trying to fit together. And each new discovery is another piece of the puzzle.

'Why would God create a different species for each island?' he asks Captain FitzRoy one evening. The captain eyes him suspiciously and says, 'Because it was his will to do so!' He had accepted a scientist on board his ship to study the flora and fauna of South America in order to confirm the biblical account of creation. '*And God saw everything that he had made, and, behold, it was very good. And the evening and the morning were the sixth day.*' Mr Darwin is a diligent scientist, but the captain finds his willingness to question everything most unorthodox.

Charles Darwin lies on his bunk, as they sail across the broad Pacific towards Australia, moving the pieces around in his head. Sometimes feeling he is on the edge of some understanding, and that if he can just let go and fall it will all come to him.

But it is not so easy to let oneself fall.

The *Beagle* sailed into Sydney Harbour on 12 January 1836, and Darwin wrote in his journal:

At last we anchored within Sydney Cove. We found the little basin occupied by many large ships, and surrounded by warehouses. In the evening I walked through the town, and returned full of admiration at the whole scene. It is a most magnificent testimony to the power of the British nation. Here, in a less promising country, scores of years have done many times more than an equal number of centuries have effected in South America. My first feeling was to congratulate myself that I was born an Englishman.

'Listen to this Mr Darwin,' says his guide, and lifting his head he shouts across the valley, 'Hello Mr Darwin!' The voice bounces back as if someone across the valley were shouting back to them.

Charles Darwin then calls, 'Hello hello!' and hears his words coming back to him, ringing around him, over and over and then fading. He doesn't like the way his words come back so clipped and distorted.

'Again,' says the guide. But Darwin isn't listening. His eyes are following the contours of the mountain cliffs around him. They stretch for many miles about the thickly wooded valley floor below. He is thinking that he will describe it in his journals as a gulf or bay, for he has only ever seen such rugged, weather-beaten cliffs by the sea.

And he wonders if the oceans had ever lapped against these cliffs. But knows that, if they did, it would have taken more than the six days of creation for the oceans to recede so many miles.

Charles Darwin found Sydney a strange place to study. He walked through the streets and the parlour rooms with the dissecting eye of a naturalist. He observed how convicts had risen to mix with people of gentry. He saw there was much prosperity. But he found that conversations among the prosperous Englishmen were limited to the topics of land and sheep.

He wrote in his journal:

The rapid prosperity and future prospects of this colony are to me, not understanding these subjects, very puzzling. The two main exports are wool and whale-oil, and to both of these productions there is a limit. The country is totally unfit for canals, therefore there is a not very distant point, beyond which the land-carriage of wool will not repay the expense of shearing and tending sheep. Pasture everywhere is so thin that settlers have already pushed far into the interior: moreover, the country further inland becomes extremely poor. Agriculture, on account of the droughts, can never succeed on an extended scale: therefore, so far as I can see, Australia must ultimately depend upon being the centre of commerce for the southern hemisphere, and perhaps on her future manufactories.

He closes his journal. The notes are not a part of the puzzle. He decides to abandon civilisation once more and strike out into the interior to see something of the nature of this new land. He hires a guide to take him over the mountains, where he is told he can expect to hunt some kangaroos or other marsupials.

He longs to shoot some of the native animals of Australia, to dissect and study them. Perhaps stuff them to take home with him. Put them in a museum case for others to study.

They ride west from Sydney, where convicts in chain gangs build the roads, and at the foot of the Blue Mountains they encounter a small band of natives. Charles Darwin stops them and for a shilling they put on an exhibition of spear throwing for him. He watches them carefully as they move. He is observing their skin colour, their hair, their skeletal structures, their faces. Studying them carefully.

Later he writes:

They were all partly clothed, and several could speak a little English: their countenances were good-humoured and pleasant, and they appeared far from being such utterly degraded beings as they have usually been represented. In their own arts they are admirable. A cap being fixed at thirty yards distance, they transfixed it with a spear, delivered by their throwing-stick with the rapidity of an arrow from the bow of a practised archer. In tracking animals or men they show most wonderful sagacity: and I heard of several of their remarks which manifested considerable acuteness. They will not however, cultivate the ground, or build houses and remain stationary, or even take the trouble of tending a flock of sheep when given to them. On the whole they appear to me to stand some few degrees higher in the scale of civilisation than the Fuegians.

And he remembers how Captain FitzRoy had told him in his initial interview that he believed firmly in the science of physiognomy. He told Darwin that he had studied his face and found the nose was too broad, indicating a lack of character. He told him how the broad, flat faces of the natives of Tierra del Fuego showed that they were the most base of God's races.

Charles Darwin wonders what the devout Captain FitzRoy would say of the faces of the natives of Australia? He thinks upon the differences in European faces. Thinks upon the similarities. And then he is thinking again about the finches. The different tiny skulls preserved in a box on the *Beagle*. Each unique. Each similar. Feels himself teetering on the edge of that abyss again.

The guide suggests he should sit down. It is a hot day. Charles Darwin is sweating heavily from the walk to the cliff's edge. He takes a seat on the sandstone rock and places his hand upon it. Feels the warmth and feels the age in it. Sees that someone has carved their name in the rock. Edward, it says. And then another near it — James. Charles Darwin is tempted for a moment to carve his own name into the sandstone. Feels some sudden need to immortalise himself in the rock.

Then his guide says, 'Do you know what I think when I see those names? That all this grand cliff face, all along here, is just God carving his name onto the landscape. Can you feel that?'

And Charles Darwin nods, for there is something breathtaking and majestic in the cliffs. Something so overwhelming that it makes him feel they could be less than men — mere beetles walking upon the earth, observed by a greater power.

All during the voyage across the Pacific, Charles Darwin's mind kept going back to the Galapagos Islands. They were like nowhere on earth he had ever seen. They were bleak and hot and overrun with grey reptiles, like some vision of hell. But they were also like Eden in a way, he thinks, for the animals there had no fear of men. The great lumbering tortoises ignored them and the birds were so tame they would almost fly into his open hands.

He took many specimens, but it was the finches that intrigued him. Thirteen different islands and 13 different finches. He thinks again of the skulls laid out in a little wooden box on the *Beagle*.

'Are there any natives in this area?' Darwin asks his guide, curious to know whether they all have the same shaped heads, or differ slightly in different locations.

'Not any more,' says the guide. 'Not since the settlers arrived in the mountains in big numbers.' Then he says, 'There was hundreds out near Bathurst, where we're heading, until only a few years back. But it's safe now. You might travel to and from there now without seeing a single black.'

And Charles Darwin makes a note for his journal: '*Wherever the European has trod, death seems to pursue the aboriginal.*'

And he wonders how many more years it might be before the race is gone altogether.

But later he writes:

> *Nor is it the white man alone that thus acts the destroyer; the Polynesian of Malay extraction has in parts of the East Indian archipelago, thus driven before him the dark-coloured native. The varieties of man seem to act on each other in the same way as different species of animals — the stronger always extirpating the weaker.*

In December 1832, the *Beagle* reached Tierra de Fuego at the extreme tip of South America. Darwin was shocked by the savageness of the natives there. Despite the bitter cold, they went about near naked, their red skins filthy and greasy.

Aboard the *Beagle* was a young missionary, Richard Matthews, and three Fuegians who had been taken to England a year earlier and civilised and educated by the Church Missionary Society. They were now returning to spread the word of God to their people.

Charles Darwin could see little similarities between them and the savages on the windswept island. He wrote in his journal:

> *How entire the difference between savage and civilised man is. — It is greater than between a wild and domesticated animal ... I believe if the world was searched, no lower grade of man could be found.*

Captain FitzRoy landed Matthews and his helpers at a site along a river and had a hut and garden built for them. They wished him well and sailed along the coast, surveying further. Upon their return ten days later, they found Matthews in fear for his life. The wild natives had besieged him, he said. They had looted all his fine linen and furnishings. He asked to return to the *Beagle*, but the three Fuegians chose to remain. Perhaps to educate their people. Perhaps to return to savagery.

The *Beagle* sailed away until the three natives seemed like nothing other than small dark rocks on the beach.

'Tell me the story about the three sisters again,' Darwin says.

And the guide tells him. 'According to the natives there were three young sisters who lived down in the valley there. Their father was a witchdoctor and knew all kinds of magic. But a bunyip lived in the valley, which is a strange kind of beast the blacks believe in, that is said to live in deep waterholes and come up at night to catch people. Bunkum really. Well, the story goes that one day the father went hunting in the valley, and he put his three daughters on an outcrop of rock over there to keep them safe from harm. But one of the daughters saw a poisonous insect and threw a large rock at it, which fell tumbling into the valley with a loud crash and woke the bunyip, and he looked up and saw the three sisters there and decided to make a meal of them. Well their father saw this from the valley floor and to save his daughters he pointed a magic bone at them and turned them to stone. But this made the bunyip wild and he ran back down the cliff to catch their father. To escape the bunyip, he turned himself into a lyrebird and hid in a small cave. But he dropped his magic bone somewhere. Maybe the bunyip took it. Maybe not. But they say when you hear the lyrebird calling it is the father, still looking for the bone. What do you think of that?'

'They believe those rocks and the animals were once human?' Charles Darwin asks.

'Oh yes,' says the guide. 'As far as I know, they say all animals and men have common ancestors.'

Charles Darwin hears the last words resounding like an echo in his head — over and over and then fading. Thinks he should take a note of it. But he feels the pull of danger again. The sacrilegiousness of the thought. Holds himself back.

He turns and studies the three large rock formations carefully. Thinks that they will still be there thousands of years after he is gone. He looks at the shape of the rock. The colours and textures. As if he were going to dissect and study them.

He has a sudden thought of the skulls of the natives laid out in a box, alongside the skulls of Europeans. Thinks it could be an important part of the puzzle.

And then a sudden updraft brings a fine spray of water up towards them. 'It is raining up,' the guide says. Darwin feels the coolness of it and stands and takes another step closer to the edge. 'Careful now sir,' says the guide. Darwin closes his eyes and holds his arms out wide. Feels the strength of the updraft. Feels the age of the sandstone beneath his feet. Thinks of God's name in it. Thinks of the natives in it.

If one of his many collected bones was a magic bone, he would become a finch, he thinks. Then he would let himself go over the edge of the abyss. But instead of falling, he would be carried up by the updraft, up and up to the heavens, where he could look down on the globe and all the races of men, and see the puzzle in its entirety. From where God sees man, he thinks, and not from where man sees God.

The Last History of Jorgen Jorgensen

Hobart Town, 1841

In the last year of his life Jorgen Jorgensen sits alone in a darkened cell, writing his final life history. This time, he swears, it will be the truth. The true exploits of Jorgen Jorgensen — sailor, explorer, whaler, liberator, protector, spy, constable and author.

He carefully lowers his pen to the blank page before him, and writes, '*Who so able to write a man's life as the living man himself?*' He pauses. Coughs up phlegm and something more solid from his lungs. Waits a moment to steady his breathing, then stares down at the page he has written. He can see nothing. Even the white paper is as black as ships' pitch in the darkened cell. Light is kept out in the belief that the darkness will both punish and rehabilitate the most recalcitrant of inmates.

Jorgen Jorgensen lowers his pen to the page again. Where to begin his story? he ponders. Where does a man's history start? At birth? At death? Or at those few moments of monumental change that determine his fate in life?

He stares into the darkness and then writes, 'Imprisonment'. For his life has been marked by terms of imprisonment.

Then he coughs and splutters again. A deep hacking cough that rakes his lungs as if the cat-o-nine-tails were being lashed across them. He fears he may not have enough time to complete his last history, but knows it is his only chance of remaining alive. Of gaining immortality.

Each word he writes will be a victory over those who slander him, he knows. Those gentlemen and historians of the colony of Van Diemens Land who refuse to recognise his greatness and grant him his place in their history. But he alone has witnessed the colony's growth over 40 years.

'I was there at its founding, and am present at its destruction,' he writes.

> In my twentieth year I sailed through Bass Strait. We were the first vessel to chart Van Diemens Land as an island. We created it for the maps of the world.
>
> Two years later, in 1802, as first mate on the *Lady Nelson*, I landed the first settlers in the colony at Risdon Cove. Then, in 1804, I travelled 28 miles up the Tamar River, aboard the *Lady Nelson*. She was an intriguing vessel, he writes, and was possessed of a moveable keel, ever changing as conditions around her changed. One moment she was a shallow-keeled boat sailing carefully through dangerous shoals, the next she lowered her keel and was running hard against the wind.
>
> At the head of the river we sighted fine land for a settlement. It made me think of my native Denmark. The land was fertile, well watered and free of natives.

Jorgen Jorgensen tries to remember if the land around Launceston really looked like Denmark. He has been away from his native land too many years, and it now exists only in his memory. One moment flat and windswept, the next rocky and hilly.

He thinks upon what he has written and guides his pen back down to the darkened paper, trying to cross out the words 'free of natives'. That came much later, he thinks.

Jorgen Jorgensen returned up the Derwent with more settlers in 1804. He stood on the ship's deck watching the settlers fell trees in the forests, carving out the first foundations of Hobart Town. He didn't see the blacks hidden there, carefully watching them, but he did see the whales. They floated thickly up the estuary and he dreamt of returning one day to hunt them.

Jorgen Jorgensen closes his eyes a moment. Listens to the sounds of the prison. Sounds from his memory. He holds his breath listening for the soft clicks and groans of metal and stone. But he cannot hold the violence within. He coughs and it echoes loudly off the walls, another racking fit that leaves him weak and shaking.

> At the age of 24 years I quit the Royal Navy and returned up the Derwent River, as chief officer on board a British whaling vessel, the *Alexander*.
>
> The estuary was filled with whales calving. We launched the longboats and began slaughtering them. By the end of two weeks the waters foamed with blood. The thick dark bodies of the black whales lay on the shores around Risdon Cove, where they were flayed, attracting seagulls and other carrion. The birds wheeled and screeched in the air, diving to the waters and fighting for morsels of blubber. The whales' blood soaked the sands.
>
> But the earth there was well used to blood. Three months previously the Risdon Cove settlement had been evacuated to Hobart Town after an attack by over 250 natives. They had advanced upon the settlers waving branches menacingly. The redcoats had opened fire on them, killing over 50.

'Their dark bodies lay on the ground, attracting birds and carrion,' he writes, and then tries to peer at the page to see if he has written that already.

Jorgen Jorgensen lifts his head and stares towards the dark wall in front of him. He imagines he is looking at his reflection. He sees an image of himself as a wild youth setting out to conquer the world. It is a prison game he has played many times over, being no stranger to prisons. He was first incarcerated by the British in 1808 as a Danish prisoner of war, despite having founded Van Diemens Land. Despite having sailed as the first

33

mate on a British vessel. Despite having established the whaling industry at Hobart.

He blinks and his reflection is gone. It is so dark in the cell that there is no difference between day and night. Jorgen Jorgensen holds his hand close in front of his face, but can see nothing. He knows that even if he were to stand close to the wall, with his face pressed up hard against the cold stone, he would still see nothing. He knows he could stand there all day staring at a single point on the wall, and it would never become any clearer.

He cannot see, he thinks, but he can remember and he can write.

> In the winter months of 1808 I was commissioned to sail a ship of supplies to Iceland. It was lighter at night than during the short days there because of the bright northern lights. Icebergs drifted slowly past in the chill currents.
>
> The Icelanders were starving on their small island. British vessels had been excluded from landing by a Danish blockade, but I braved the northern oceans and sailed a ship of grain into Reykjavik harbour. I was so overwhelmed by the need of the inhabitants that I immediately returned to the port of Liverpool for more supplies. But upon my return to Iceland I found all British ships had been prohibited, by proclamation of the Danish governor!
>
> So I carefully watched the natives on shore from the deck of my vessel, and when they had gone into church on Sunday morning I went directly to the governor's residence, with a small armed party, and deposed him. By the time the church service was over and the citizens reappeared, the Danish governor was safely on board my ship and I was safely ensconced as their new Danish ruler.
>
> I began my rule by cutting taxes, increasing public salaries and opening up trade with Britain. The natives of Iceland

> praised me as their saviour. They gave me the title of
> Protector.
>
> I toured my new realm and was benevolent to my subjects,
> only having to threaten one farmer with burning his farm
> for refusing to recognise my title. I was well suited to the
> position of protector. But I slept ill at nights. The strange
> lava rock formations of Iceland, in the dim evenings,
> appeared to me like hostile troops, biding their time before
> attacking.
>
> But they were waiting for me in London. Upon my return
> to England later in 1809, I was arrested on the charge of
> breaking my parole as a prisoner of war, and sentenced to
> transportation.

Jorgen Jorgensen cocks his head and listens. On some nights he can hear the distant wails as the skin is flayed off some prisoner. And on other nights he suddenly wakes up with a start, and realises that he's been dreaming of Iceland again. Dreaming of being king of that craggy island, where the spirits of the dead lived in the rocks and lava formations, silently watching him. Where the people called him protector and saviour, but never one of them.

> My darkest years were from 1817 to 1820, when gambling
> entered my bloodstream. Floating into my veins like
> icebergs. Chilling my reason and filling me with a
> murderous passion. A need to conquer and win. I spent long
> nights and days imprisoned in the gambling dens of
> London, betting everything on the fall of the dice.
>
> How subtle are the twists of fortune. The fickle fall of a
> dice can change a man's life in an instant. One moment
> edging forward carefully over the dangerous shoals, the
> next running hard against the wind. The rolling dice of fate
> tumble beneath you, and you wake up one day a king, the
> next a prisoner.

> In my fortieth year I was convicted of stealing bedclothes to
> sell to pay off my gambling debts. The penalty, I was
> warned, could be death. I protested that I was a loyal
> servant of the king! They said I was a foreign provocateur.
> I said I had once been a king. They said I was a
> revolutionary. I said I had reported for the king at
> Waterloo. They said I was a spy.
>
> I was sentenced to be transported to Van Diemens Land!

Jorgen Jorgensen wakes up with a start. Is it another day already? In the darkness he does not know if he has slept for minutes or days. He had been dreaming of the past again. He stares fixedly at the cell wall. As if he can see something there. And he remembers Waterloo. He remembers strolling across the blood-soaked fields, wondering what turned men to such violence? How did men live with the knowledge that they had slaughtered their fellow men like they were so much game?

And then he remembers the blood-soaked fields of Van Diemens Land. Riding with the roving parties upon his release from prison. Hunting down the wild blacks.

'They said the blacks would die if they were locked up,' he writes. They could not stand the confines of a cell. They would die if confined.

Jorgen Jorgensen understands this. He too is a man who needs space. The whole world has been his nation. And he remembers standing on the decks of the *Lady Nelson*, carefully watching the blacks watching the first settlers at Hobart. They carried spears and moved slowly through the trees. And he remembers thinking he would return one day and hunt them.

Now Van Diemens Land is free of natives and he dreams of sailing a ship of supplies to their small prison mission on Flinders Island to the north. Of deposing the governor. Of being their protector. Their saviour.

This time, he swears, it will be the truth.

And he thinks of the blacks at Risdon Cove. He knows about their attack. Over the years he has recorded the customs and languages of the blacks. He knows enough of their ways to know that they had not been attacking the settlers, but encircling kangaroos in a hunt. They had been driving them towards the shore, waving green branches as they proceeded onwards. Harmless to the settlers. Then the redcoats opened fire.

If he had been there he could have saved them, he thinks. They would have called him their saviour. The King of Van Diemens Land.

Jorgen Jorgensen looks down at the pages he has written. Tries to read the words. Tries to read his history. It is like trying to see the dark stone wall in front of him. Like trying to read the future. He closes his eyes and in the stillness he feels that he could be the last man alive on earth, turning slowly to stone. Dreaming of the years when he was still alive.

'This time it will be the truth,' he writes.

> My greatest exploration and discovery was during the black wars. I was employed at the rank of constable to ride with the roving parties, hunting the wild blacks in the interior of the colony. Each month we reported that despite seeing the smoke of several fires and glimpsing the blacks at a distance, we had been unable to capture any of them. Yet I remember their bodies lying thickly on the ground.

Jorgen Jorgensen lifts his pen from the page. He wants to write that he saved the blacks. That he was their protector. But all he writes is, 'their blood soaked the earth'.

Jorgen Jorgensen coughs. A long racking cough. He listens to the echo it makes in his small cell. It sounds to him like the distant wail as a prisoner's skin is flayed. Not long now, he thinks, and feels the chill of the stone walls spreading into his body. He is turning to stone, he thinks. He coughs again. There is a chill in his lungs like the wind off the icebergs that drift north from Antarctica. Floating slowly through his veins like large pale whales, drifting through his memory. Lying bloody on the shores. Dark bodies lying thickly in the bush. The birds diving and fighting. Picking over scraps and bones.

He turns a new page. I have written the past, he thinks, and now I will write the future. He carefully guides his pen to the page.

'I will be released from gaol soon,' he writes.

I will be given a new appointment as protector of the blacks. I will write their history. I will write their languages and customs and keep them alive. Historians will find it and will proclaim it as the greatest treatise on the blacks of Van Diemens Land. Jorgen Jorgensen Land they will come to call it. And one hundred and fifty years from now people will flock to this cell to see where I wrote my last great history. Where I saved the blacks.

He closes his eyes and tries to see it. But all he can see are the dark bodies still drifting through his memory. He opens his eyes and stares at the wall and for an instant he can see his own reflection drifting with them. Watching them. He feels the rolling dice of fate turning beneath him. Turning against him. Carrying him into the dangerous shoals once more.

He stops. Crosses out all he has written. 'This time the truth,' he writes.

Sorry Business

Port Phillip, 1842

'You sorry fellows,' says George Augustus Robinson, staring down at the empty graves. Waiting patiently for the bodies to arrive. He is glad he has not attended the hanging. He saw too many of his blacks die while he was commandant of the Wybalenna mission in Van Diemens Land. These two more deaths make him both sad and angry. 'They should be very sorry for this,' he mutters. 'Very sorry indeed.'

He does not need to attend the hanging to know what it will be like. A huge crowd of several thousand will be pushing and shoving to get a look at the gallows. Turned out like they were attending a royal picnic. Standing on walls and sitting on shoulders to get a decent — or an indecent — view.

The two black men, dressed in coarse white, will be led up onto the platform. They will look around themselves in fear and desperation. So many people. So much noise. But they will look for him. Hoping that he might appear and save them, for he had always promised that he would protect them. But he is not there. And the sudden fear of dying in a strange land will make their legs shake and quiver.

The preacher will begin the prayers, and some in the crowd will call on him to get on with it. Then the death masks will be pulled over the two men's faces and the nooses fastened around their necks. The crowd will fall silent then. When death is so close it is not easily made light of.

But the gallows will malfunction and Maulboyheener, who the locals know as Timmy, will not fall cleanly. The rope will snag and he will be dangling there alive. Kicking and struggling frantically. His chained legs flailing wildly up in the air, trying desperately to seek some imaginary toe-hold that could save his life, but there is none. His legs will gradually slow. Then twitch slightly. Then hang still.

The gruesome struggle will have shocked the crowd. They will stare in silent fascination, waiting for the second man to be hanged. His will be much cleaner. Pevay will fall well and hit the end of the rope with a clean jerk. Hanging limply. Swaying slightly in the breeze. Lifeless.

Then the crowd will look about expectantly, as if waiting for somebody to take up a cheer or something. But nothing else happens. Then they slowly disperse, walking back to their homes, or to their labours, replaying the scene of the hanging over in their minds, so that one day, many years from now, they can retell it to their families or grandchildren. Just as it happened from their differing points of view.

'Let me tell you about the day they hanged the murderous Van Diemens Land blacks,' they will say.

The bodies of the two dead men are transported to the Aboriginal graveyard in George Augustus Robinson's own cart. He has volunteered to conduct the funeral rites. He is long practised at reading the words at the funerals of his blacks.

The cart is accompanied by the other Van Diemens Land blacks. Trugernanna, Wooredy and the rest. They are weeping openly. As the bodies are unloaded George Augustus Robinson, Chief Protector of Aborigines of Port Phillip, moves across and puts one arm around Trugernanna, his old companion of many years. His precious black princess, who has helped him in his work for so many years. Trugernanna, whom he thought he knew and understood so intimately, yet whom he was shocked to find himself defending to Superintendent La Trobe on charges of murder. He feels hurt by this. Wants her to make amends to him.

George Augustus Robinson, brickmaker turned saviour, lifts Trugernanna's face. 'It's over,' he says. Then, 'They were ungrateful wretches and will be sorry for this.'

Trugernanna pushes his arm away and falls to the ground beside her dead countrymen. He takes a step away from her. She has hurt him again. He will ask her to apologise later, but for now he dare not confront her, a man from the press is edging closer and George Augustus Robinson is already fearful of what he might write about him.

George Augustus Robinson has tried to talk with Trugernanna, but she has remained silent and obstinate in the face of his kindness.

He is greatly relieved to hear that Superintendent La Trobe has agreed to repatriate the remaining Van Diemens Land blacks to the Wybalenna mission on Flinders Island. He is pleased they are going back, as he is pleased that he is no longer the commandant there. Port Phillip has so much more promise for him, he thinks.

He told Trugernanna that she would be going home again. She said he was lying. That they would be sent back to Flinders Island. He insisted that that was their home. That there was no more home for them on the Van Diemens Land mainland. She said nothing, but refused to let him touch her.

He does not know what to do with her any more. He feels he does not know her any more. He is glad to consign her and her people to the past. Of the 15 Aboriginal charges he brought over to the mainland, already six have died. It is time for them all to go.

George Augustus Robinson sits up late with his journal open on the desk before him. He writes obsessively. He has no desire to go to bed this evening. He is distant from his wife again. The stories in his journals are always kinder than the whispers and slanders being recorded against him across the colonies. They say he is a fraud. That he has misappropriated official funds and supplies. That he has had improper relations with his charges. That he has removed skulls of the dead. They are calling for an official inquiry into the Wybalenna mission on Flinders Island. But they do not know him. They begrudge him a few luxuries to supplement his meagre salary. They do not know what great feats he achieved in his earlier years.

If they could only read of those years in the wilderness, as recorded in his diaries, they would know him them. Except those intimate secrets only recorded in Trugernanna's tongue. He leans back in his chair as if reading those memories. The Great Conciliator they had called him after he had single-handedly gone to face the wild natives and had brought them into the mission. They had said he was mad when he announced his intent. But he had shown them all his greatness.

His pen is poised in the air. How to put the words just right? he ponders. How to put the words so they look as if they've flowed freely out of his fertile mind down though his arm and into his pen?

He thinks upon this very carefully each day as he writes down in his journal the vast adventures and achievements that constitute his life. Some day, he thinks, people will dig up his body and probe it for his secrets. And they will also dig up his journals. Petty men and historians will try to diminish his greatness, searching for scandal. Trying to support the lies they already tell about him.

So he thinks very carefully before ever committing his pen to paper. Thinks back on his years as conciliator of the blacks, travelling across Van Diemens Land to bring the wild blacks into civilisation — and then to his promotion to commandant of the blacks at the mission station on Flinders Island in the Bass Strait — and now finally as Chief Protector of the Aborigines at Port Phillip. His journals have grown to several large books and cover many thousands of pages. Yet every word in them is carefully considered. They will not find in them anything to support the whispers and slanders made against him.

One day he will write his own history of the colonies, he thinks, revealing to the world the crucial role he has played in establishing their prosperity. Revealing his vast knowledge of the blacks and their customs. Reminding an easily forgetting world of the role he played in averting violence and death.

He closes his eyes for a moment and sees himself as an elderly gentlemen, sitting in a large living room in London. Eminent men of science and young women of high society are gathered around him. And when he turns to address them it is in deep rich tones, with not a trace of his east end working-class accent.

'They called me the Great Conciliator,' he says, as the men and women listen attentively. 'I walked out alone into the wilderness of the colony, into the very heart of the wild black tribes, fearless of their spears and sharp axes, and playing upon my flute, like a modern pied piper, I tamed and civilised them, brought them in from the wilderness and educated them. Preached to them the benefits of Christianity. Converted them to God's ways. Ended the conflict and introduced them to British civilisation.'

The men and women around him are awed. But he looks out the window and sighs. Tells them that sometimes he misses his years spent in the colony. Misses the challenges of those years. Sometimes he even misses his wife and children, who have stayed behind on his vast estates there.

He opens his eyes and looks down at his journal. He sighs again. Sometimes he does miss those years spent travelling in the wilderness. The adventure of it. Danger and Trugernanna were his constant companions. If only she'd never turned away from him, he thinks. If only so many things had turned out differently.

He looks out the window. It is dark outside. Rain is running down the glass. He can see his reflection in the glass. A dark vision of himself. With water running down his face like tears. He wonders how many other blacks might die tonight? Wonders what to write of the departure of the last Van Diemens Land blacks? It might be the last time he sees Trugernanna, he thinks. He wishes she would apologise to him before she goes. He decides to write the date and departure details only. And the fact that Wooredy is ill and George Augustus Robinson doubts he will last the voyage back. Wooredy seems to know it himself.

That would prove a dry enough bone for the later grave robbers and historians to pick over, he thinks.

He presses his pen to the page and writes a line before realising that the ink in his pen has dried up and he is scratching blankly across the page.

When Trugernanna arrived at the colony of Port Phillip with George Augustus Robinson, she shocked him, her protector, by taking to the bush. By sleeping openly with local natives or with white men. He admonished her. Told her that he expected her and the other blacks to help him civilise the Port Phillip natives. But instead they took to the bush. Went on their robbing and murder rampage.

It was done to hurt him personally, he knew.

At the court case he had defended her against the charge of murder by stating that she had once saved his life in the wild and had never lacked in humanity. He told the court how she had assisted him in the interior of Van Diemens Land. How she had taught him the ways of the blacks, taught him their beliefs, taught him her tongue. She was so young and lively then, he remembers. An impish smile ever on her lips. Her lithe dark body ever keen to guide and please him.

He sighs and looks back out the window beyond his reflection, into the darkness. They were the best days of his life, he thinks. He was young, strong, confident. The whole world was before him. Armed with only his faith and self-confidence he strode into the wild interior of Tasmania to conduct intercourse with the blacks there.

After she had been released from gaol into his care, he had asked Trugernanna what had ever become of those days. She had glared at him insolently. They had never existed except in his own memory, she told him.

George Augustus Robinson was near weeping with rage. In all his years as commandant of the Wybalenna mission on Flinders Island, the natives have rarely seen him so angry. He had them assembled in the brick chapel. He had overseen its construction himself. Proof of his dedication to his charges. Another black had died. Another! His anger left him speechless for a moment. One more grave to be dug and one more funeral service to be prepared. There were less than 80 of the race left.

'What has happened is intolerable,' he said to the natives, raising his voice as if he were addressing a large auditorium. 'The deaths must not continue!' He looked about him, then went on. Still shouting. 'I am the Commandant of the Aborigine Settlement,' he said. 'If you all die, what will I be then? Nothing! You should all be sorry for the way you are treating me!'

Nobody said anything for a time. Then Trugernanna said, 'We want to return to our homeland.'

George Augustus Robinson calmed a little. 'I acknowledge that you grieve for your homeland,' he said. 'But that is the past and has nothing to do with the present. They were different times.'

Again nobody said anything. They just stared at him, unmoving. He appeared a very small man to them, as if standing a very long way from them. And yet the past did not seem so very far away at all.

And then, led by Trugernanna, the blacks all stood and turned their backs on him.

'You will be very, very sorry!' he said. Much softer.

The first George Augustus Robinson, Chief Protector of the Aborigines of Port Phillip, knew of the rampage of his blacks was when he received word that two whalers had been murdered at nearby Cape Patterson. Trugernanna, with two women and two men, had left the settlement and they were heading east, robbing and burning homesteads. They had stolen several guns and had also stolen £22 in bank notes — which they had wantonly burned.

The police, he was told, assisted by black trackers, were on their trail, pursuing them as he himself had once pursued the wild blacks in Van Diemens Land.

George Augustus Robinson put his head in his hands when told. The press would link them to him. The governor would demand an inquiry. His pension would be in jeopardy. He sat there alone in his study and wondered what to do. This would be harder than dealing with the natives who had died at Wybalenna or on the Port Phillip Protectorate. You could not hide white bodies from the press.

He knew what they would write:

Information has been received in town that numerous depredations have been committed in the Westernport direction by a party of the Aborigines accompanied by and associated with two Van Diemen's Land blacks and three women who are as well skilled in the use of the firearms they possess as the males.

These peoples have been imported by Mr Robinson for the purpose of aiding in the civilization of the Aborigines of Australia Felix.

George Augustus Robinson looks up from his journal and peers out his study window. It is still dark outside and he cannot see the future there.

He has heard that deaths on Flinders Island have continued in his absence. Like the progress on the inquiry. But they will not be able to blame him for those deaths. He is well to be out of it, he thinks. Although he will miss Trugernanna. And he wishes for a moment that he might have had her with him, hunting down the other Van Diemens Land blacks when they ran away. Together they might have brought them in peacefully, as they had brought in the wild Big River and Ben Lomond tribes so many years before.

They would call him the Great Conciliator again then. Praise him greatly. Increase his pension and salary. But he is no longer the Great Conciliator. He is now the Chief Protector. And he knows that he has failed to protect anyone.

His journals will never record that though. As they will never record the truth about his time in the wilds with Trugernanna. That is the past, he thinks.

The first unwritten time was in the Van Diemens Land highlands when they were hunting down the Big River Tribe. He was growing more and more concerned as they progressed deeper and deeper into the wilderness. It was apparent the Big River Tribe knew they were after them and seemed to be toying with them. They would light fires so that he could see the smoke, but by the time he reached their campsite it would be deserted. His own tame blacks were very nervous and kept saying, 'They near now. Very near.'

George Augustus Robinson suspected the Big River Tribe were hiding in the bush around them, watching their vain efforts to catch them. They were renowned for their violence and had killed several settlers on outlying properties. The thought of their sharp spears turned his bowels to water, but he kept on. Back then he had still had strong faith in the Lord and was driven by the promise of the £700 he would receive for bringing in the last of them. Even then he had had the dream of sitting in an English drawing room as a man of wealth and position.

His strategy to win over the wild blacks had been to send his tame blacks into their camp, naked, and they would talk to them and tell them he was coming to save them. To protect them from the guns of the soldiers. To take them to a safe place. When they agreed to this he would be signalled to come forward. He had won them over, he would write in his journal, by the sheer force of his will.

And now he was pushing deeper and deeper into the Big River Tribe's territory, following closely behind Trugernanna, who, naked, kept repeating softly, 'They near now. Very near.'

George Augustus Robinson was sweating heavily. Blood was pounding in his ears. He could not rid his mind of the fear. The thought of those sharpened hidden spears. Thrusting suddenly out of the bushes. Penetrating his flesh. Stabbing him over and over. He tried to concentrate only on Trugernanna in front of him. Watched the strong muscles in her buttocks. Saw the faint wisp of hair that peeped out between her legs when she took a long step. Concentrated on the curve of her skin. The shape of her breast as she turned her flank sideways.

If only she weren't a black, he had often thought to himself, as they sat close by the campfire at night. And then later, if only she wasn't quite so black. But her skin was black now, coated in sweat and moisture from the forest, and it looked more beautiful than anything he had ever seen. Instead of thinking of the sharpened spears of the Big River Tribe, he was suddenly thinking only of the closeness of Trugernanna. Blood pounding in his ears. He was sweating heavily. Thinking of spearing her where she walked.

He stopped, suddenly short of breath. Trugernanna turned to look at him.

'We very close now,' she said. He took a step forward. Stumbled. Fell into her arms. Held her tightly. Fell to the earth, taking her with him. Rolling on the rocky ground. Fumbling to free himself. Striving to hold her. Thrusting and penetrating her savagely. Over and over and over.

His legs began shaking. His pale buttocks quivering uncontrollably. Then his mind cleared a little and he looked closely at Trugernanna pinned beneath him. He wanted to say something. Something appropriate. But of course there were no words.

Then Trugernanna said something in his ear. He heard the word 'Big'. He nodded. Then 'River'. Yes it was like a river. Then 'Tribe!'. It was as if he had been struck by a war club. He fumbled with his trousers. Rolling away over the rocky ground towards the bushes. Away from the Big River Tribe's sharp spears. Away from their sharp gaze, watching his white buttocks vanish into the shrubbery.

He thought the Big River people were going to kill him, but they went with him to the mission on Flinders Island. And they were the ones who were dead now.

George Augustus Robinson sits up with a shock. As if his body has suddenly been jolted at the end of a rope. He looks around, expecting to see a large empty grave, but sees by the early morning light that he is sitting in the chair in his study. He has fallen asleep there. He was having a dream. He had been standing by the empty graves on the day of the hangings. But one was his grave. He had been digging his own grave. And he was standing in it, staring at a photograph in his hands. A photograph of Trugernanna. A picture of her in her last year of life. As the last of her race.

No, that would not be quite right, he thinks. There would still be those natives who lived with the sealers in the strait islands, those who had resisted being taken to the Flinders Island mission. Those who had never been his blacks and had never existed in his history.

He closes his eyes and tries to remember the photograph of Trugernanna — his black princess. In the dream of the photograph she had become an old woman, thickset with heavy limbs, short grey hair, heavy features and a small wispy beard under her chin. And her forehead was wrinkled into a frown of concern. As if she knew how little time she had left to live. As Wooredy had known.

But it is the eyes that he can most recall. They were dark and accusing, staring slightly away from the photographer. Staring into the past perhaps. Or staring at him.

He is suddenly afraid of what she is saying about him. Eventually, he imagines, others may see this photograph of her and, after her death, read in her eyes what she knew of him. All the secrets she refused to reveal in life.

He then has a terrible realisation: after he dies he will be unable to defend himself in his journals, but through her photograph she will keep living. And her accusations will live with her.

George Augustus Robinson suddenly feels very sorry for himself. He knows he has always been concerned about the future of the blacks, but he also knows that he has been more concerned about what history will say of him. He has defended himself in his journals, repeatedly, saying he had asked for more funding, tried to build new mission stations. But it was the blacks who kept dying. Undermining his efforts.

He feels very sorry indeed about the way things turned out. His promises to the Big River and Ben Lomond tribes. The deaths on Flinders Island. The hangings in Port Phillip. And Trugernanna.

There were so many promises.

He sits in front of his journal and he wishes he could write it all better again. But he doesn't know what words might fix it.

Suddenly there is a light knock on the door and his wife Maria peeps in. She sees him sitting in his chair, holding up a photograph that isn't there. Staring at it fixedly.

She wonders whether to disturb him or not, then asks, 'Did you have a message to send to the blacks before they sail?'

'Sorry?' he says.

The Unknown South Land

Het Onbekende Zuidland, 1629

Jan Pelgrom kneels in the sand weeping as the ship sails away towards the distant western horizon. If he could get to his feet he would run into the water after it.

'They'll come back for us, won't they?' he sobs. His voice is clogged with snot and tears. 'Won't they?' But the elder man beside him doesn't answer. Wouter Loos saves his words in order to curse the devil that has led them to be condemned to a life in this godforsaken unknown land. He turns from the ocean and walks away up the beach, tying a large kerchief around his head, like the Dutch peasants did. His eyes are fixed inland. 'Our future is this way now,' he says, more to himself than to Jan, who stays by the ocean's edge, wiping desperately at the tears in his eyes, trying to keep the receding ship in sight.

Terra Australis Incognita, 1846

Fathers Salvado and Serra are the first of the Benedictine monks to step ashore at Fremantle. The colony is barely 17 years old, and seems to have an air of temporariness still about it. The unfamiliar stillness of the land is a joy to them after the long ocean voyage from Italy. The creak of ropes and timbers has accompanied them halfway around the world. Father Salvado plants his feet firmly in the sand and then falls to his knees. He calls his fellow black-robed Benedictines to his side. 'We will praise Almighty God for delivering us safely to this new world. And with His help we will tread this land in the name of the Almighty, bringing His word to the natives.'

And with tears of joy running down his face he begins singing a Latin hymn of praise to his lord and protector. *Deo gratias*.

Het Onbekende Zuidland

Jan Pelgrom is reluctant to venture so far from the beach. All their provisions are there. Their food and water. And the valuable wooden toys given to them by Commodore Pelsaert for trading with the natives. But Wouter Loos says that, if they do not leave the beach and search for the people of this land, their provisions will quickly run out.

Jan Pelgrom knows what he means. He has seen the violent excesses that fighting for food and water can bring. After the wreck of their ship *Batavia* he had watched men turn to savages. He has seen how easily the devil could come amongst them and tempt them. He has followed the devil himself and has shed blood to obtain drinking water.

He follows Wouter Loos's heavy footsteps across the dry landscape, glad that he had escaped a capital sentence on the gallows for his part in the mutiny. But now he wonders if he has only prolonged the suffering and inevitability of his death.

Terra Australis Incognita

Father Rosendo Salvado pauses to wipe the sweat from his brow. It is running down his face, making it difficult to see far ahead. But his vision is strong.

His four brother Benedictines stop beside him, glad he has slowed his pace a little today. The young Frenchman, Brother Fonteinne, turns and looks back over his shoulder. It has been over ten days since they left Perth and there is no longer the slightest hint of civilisation behind them. They are well and truly in the wilderness now. Perhaps beyond where any white man has ever trodden, he thinks.

Father Salvado sits down and opens his notebook. There is a word he sees on one of the pages. *Maragna*, the first word spoken to him by one of the natives in Perth. He had to ask the settlers there what it meant. Food, he was told. But in his own Galician dialect the same word meant deception.

Brother Fonteinne wants to ask Father Salvado how long they will walk until they reach the site of their mission, but he knows what he will say — that Christ spent 40 days and nights in the wilderness and that they should not expect to do any less.

But he also knows that Christ encountered the devil in the wilderness, and he fears that he will not prove as strong when the devil tempts and torments him.

Het Onbekende Zuidland

The two Dutchmen have walked for over ten days and encountered nothing but dry wasteland, until they spy the distant thin column of smoke. Their first sign of hope.

Jan Pelgrom is expectant, his thin gangly limbs flapping in excitement. He vividly recalls the tales of the natives of the Spice Islands. He believes they will be fed and treated well by the natives in this land. Given silk clothes to wear, and gold and silver ornaments. Dancing maidens will lie with them while others fetch cool drinks of exotic fruits.

But as they draw closer they can see only five lone men ahead of them. Thin, naked and black. They have no riches. No houses. Just a small pitiful fire. They stand regarding the two white men silently. Their tall spears stretching high above their heads. Like dark shadows of men.

'What should we do?' asks Jan Pelgrom, suddenly afraid. 'We must ask them to give us food and water.' But he realises they have nothing to trade. For an instant he thinks of running all the way back to the beach to get the wooden toys and mirrors. 'They would take us to their cities,' he says. 'Treat us like kings.'

'Be still,' says Wouter Loos quietly. He knows there will be no cities. Knows they are not going to be treated like kings. Perhaps Commodore Pelsaert had known it too when he spared their lives for their part in the mutiny and murders of the *Batavia* survivors. Perhaps he had known it when he read out their sentences, banishing them to the unknown south land. Proclaiming that they should trade with the locals and attempt to procure gems and gold and rare spices. Perhaps he had known it when he promised them that, by establishing commercial links for the almighty Dutch East India Company, they might achieve some atonement for their heinous crimes.

'Be still and wait,' Wouter Loos commands Jan, and sits down in the dirt, pulling the thin young man with him. 'If they wish to slay us they will slay us. If they wish to help us they will help us.'

Jan begins crying again, and Wouter Loos says, 'Your breath would be better spent in praying that the savages will spare our lives.'

But Jan, who has followed the devil, and has murdered and blasphemed, feels that God is no longer with him. He feels that if there is truly any place on earth close to hell then he has now reached it. And as he cries his tears fall to the dry earth and are quickly absorbed into the dust.

Terra Australis Incognita

Again Father Salvado falls to his knees. Their first task is to pray on the site of their chosen mission. Then they will erect a hut. The five Benedictines, well used to the hard work prescribed by their order, cut timber and dig holes. They work joyously, trimming the wood and fixing it together. Erecting shelter and digging the dry hard earth. They toil in the midday heat, but all the while imagining they are praying in the coolness of a tall stone cathedral.

The Benedictines — two Spanish fathers; Brother Tootle, the Englishman; Brother Fonteinne, the Frenchman; and John Gorman, the Irish catechist — only share Latin and some English as a common tongue, but all are united in devotion to their task.

Towards evening they pause to admire their work. Silently proud of their progress. Father Serra is the first to see the natives. About a dozen of them. Cautious in the distance. Watching them.

Brother Fonteinne closes his eyes and prays. The others watch his lips moving. Silently. They know he has feared this moment. Expects the natives will fall upon them and slaughter them. He has heard the stories of the French missionaries working in Northern America. He will suffer a similar martyrdom, he believes.

But the natives sit and build a fire. Carefully watching the five black-robed men.

Het Onbekende Zuidland

Jan Pelgrom sleeps fitfully. He is convinced that death is near to him. He fears the natives. Fears this unknown land. He can feel death stalking him in the darkness. Reaching out to grasp his heart and bowels and rip them from his body.

It is an awful chill feeling that he has felt before, when the commodore sentenced him to be hung for the murders and rapes he had committed on the small islands they came to call the Batavia's Graveyard. But then he had thrown himself at the commodore's feet, crying for forgiveness, begging for mercy, begging to be spared death. Begging for his life.

And at night his own pitiful words come back to him, mixed with the screams and pleas of those he had mercilessly slain at the command of the undermerchant of the flagship *Batavia*. Self-appointed supreme commander of the mutineers. The devil incarnate.

He whispers the devil's name. Says it for the first time since reaching this strange land, 'Jeronimus Cornelisz'. And immediately he wishes he had not said it, wishes he had not introduced that name to this land. And then, despite the heat of the night, he shivers the length of his body.

Terra Australis Incognita

Brother Fonteinne lies awake, listening expectantly for the soft footfalls of the natives stalking them. Spears poised to gut them. He jumps at each sound in the night. But finally, near dawn, he drifts off to sleep.

But he is the first awake in the morning. Sitting up suddenly — screaming and shouting. The brothers leap to their feet in alarm, the screaming filling their ears. The sound of a thousand tortured souls crying in alarm and pain.

They look up and see a thick cloud of white cockatoos circling over their heads, screeching loud enough to crack the dry earth.

They also see that the natives are gone.

Het Onbekende Zuidland

Jan Pelgrom and Wouter Loos are walking with the natives. Trailing along behind them with their dogs. Jan protests that he cannot keep up and Wouter Loos has to assist him. He tells him repeatedly to keep quiet. Tells him not to annoy the blacks. Tells him that they are not going to kill them and eat them.

'But we are going further from the ocean,' says Jan. 'How will we see the ships when they return for us?' Wouter Loos does not reply.

'Commodore Pelsaert said ships would make for the south land and we should contact them with smoke signs,' says Jan, pleading.

Wouter Loos grabs Jan's head and turns it to face his own. Stares into his eyes. 'We are probably the only white men to have ever set foot on this land. Why should we expect others will follow?'

'They will follow,' says Jan. 'And they will find us.'

'Perhaps,' says Wouter Loos. 'But I don't think it will be in our lifetimes.'

Jan Pelgrom squeezes his eyes shut. As if he is going to start crying again. But instead he says, 'I wish I was strong like you. I wish I could endure like you. I know the commodore had to torture you repeatedly before you confessed to your murders.'

And Wouter Loos releases his hold on Jan Pelgrom. Drops him to the dirt. Says, 'Never talk of that time again!' Then he strides off, leaving the younger man to walk for himself. Jan calls out for him to come back, to help him. Tells him he loves him. Tells him he hates him. Watches him walk further and further away from him.

Terra Australis Incognita

Father Salvado and Father Serra are walking with the natives. A little further from their mission each day. Slowly winning their confidence. Carrying their small children on their shoulders. Sharing their own food with them. And sharing in return their catch of lizards and grubs. They smile broadly and think of John the Baptist living on locusts as they force the crackling insects into their mouths.

Father Salvado has grown thin and weary, but he will not let the blacks leave him behind. Knows he must keep up with them if he is to be accepted by them, if he is to work with them. To spread God's word to them.

The key will be in words, he thinks. And each time the natives teach him a new word he stops to write it down in a small notebook he carries.

Turi is a footprint, he writes. *Pirca* is to be sick. *Uaindalco* is to fear.

Het Onbekende Zuidland

Jan Pelgrom has not seen the ocean for many weeks and he wonders if he will ever see it again. He remembers how it had haunted him on the isle of the Batavia's Graveyard. He'd dreamt it was rising over them at night and drowning them all. And he thinks back to the long days of hell on those chill dry islands, scanning the sky for any promise of rain. Wandering around and around the rocks in the vain hope of finding a freshwater pool.

He has begun learning the natives' language and at nights, around the campfires, he tells them stories of his terrible time on the islands of the dead.

He recalls how Jeronimus Cornelisz was washed ashore on the spar of the ship's mast. He thinks now that, if they had only recognised him as the devil then, they could have bound him to that mast and erected it high over the island, crucifying him there.

'The devil came to us fastened onto a beam,' he says, 'We thought him dead, but he returned to us.'

Terra Australis Incognita

Father Salvado has been progressing well with the natives' language. He has compiled a long vocabulary and uses it to recount tales from scripture to them. One evening, sitting around a campfire, he tells the story of Christ healing the sick. How God's power helped him perform miracles.

The natives nod. They have seen the Benedictines cure people they had thought close to death. They understand this power.

The natives listen readily to his stories. They are quick to point out similarities to their own stories. Father Salvado listens to them carefully to learn the beliefs that control their lives, like the cycles of the land. 'They believe in a God and a devil,' he tells his brother Benedictines. 'They believe that when a person dies, his soul is born in another person.'

Father Serra smiles. 'It would be good to think that the work of our short lives would be continued by another generation.'

'One day Christ will be reborn amongst us,' says Father Salvado to the natives. 'He died on a cross that we might be saved. Evil men whipped him and tortured him and then killed him. Hung him upon a cross. And the sky went dark like night and a mighty roar filled the people's ears as the earth shook. He died. But he will return from the clouds of heaven to save us.'

Het Onbekende Zuidland

'The deaths began in stealth,' says Jan Pelgrom, staring into the campfire. Staring far away. 'Jeronimus Cornelisz's warriors took their victims to nearby islands. And murdered them there. Or drowned them in the deep waters of the oceans. Then they returned and told the tribe that their food and water would last better if they were spread across several islands. But the cries of the dying carried across in the night. Red stains in the ocean seeped into our dreams. We knew what was happening, but we would not say it. We feared to say it. If a person disappeared in the night no-one would say their name again. As if they had ceased to be. Had never been.'

'Then the devil grew bolder. He had his warriors creep around the shelters at night and call out the names of their victims. Call them out into the night. Out into the darkness. From where they would never return.'

'No-one dared sleep,' he says. 'Waiting fearfully for the devil to call their name.'

The natives nod. They know the stories of the devil that stalks them in the darkness.

'And still the devil grew bolder,' says Jan. 'One noonday a man was killed in broad daylight. Chased into the ocean and slain. He would have drowned himself in his terror had they not caught him at the water's edge and hacked him to death with their swords.'

He tells them how the devil, Jeronimus Cornelisz, turned the survivors of the *Batavia* shipwreck against each other in daily acts of bloodshed. How he laughed when they killed at his command.

But he does not tell them how he had decided to avoid becoming one of the devil's victims — by becoming one of his followers. How he had chased the man into the ocean as he ran, begging and pleading for mercy. But Jan kept swinging awkwardly at him with the heavy sword. Eager to kill to please the devil.

Terra Australis Incognita

Father Salvado has a dream. Upon waking he shares it with his brothers. He sweeps his hand in a broad arc, taking in their small rough hut and few meagre crops, and he tells them that it will one day be the site of a major monastery. Stone buildings and a large church: a tribute to the Lord, a safe haven for the natives. An oasis of God's peace amongst a harsh and violent land.

'But the natives are nomadic,' says Father Serra. 'How will you entreat them to change their lives?'

'Their lives changed the day we arrived here,' Father Salvado replies.

Het Onbekende Zuidland

Wouter Loos has been very ill for many days. Unable to walk. There is a great pain in his heart and intestines. Jan Pelgrom has stayed by his side. Wishes he knew how to cure him. Wishes he could remember some prayers or a passage from scripture that could heal him. He tells Wouter that they must keep up with the tribe or they will die. Wouter Loos does not answer. He is already dead.

But Jan will not let him die. He fears death. He tries to goad Wouter to open his eyes to him. Whispers forbidden stories into his ears. Tells him how he remembers the murders he had committed for Jeronimus Cornelisz. Tells him of the first time they had been invited into his tent and shown his jewels and rich clothes, and how he had given them food and a chalice of wine and a sharp sword and told them to go out and kill those he had named.

Jan repeats the names of each one they had slain. 'Andries de Vries was the first,' he says. 'And there were the two women, Janneken Gist and Anneken Hardens. And then Cornelis Alderszschans, who was only a boy, and there was another younger boy on the far island. I hacked him to death.'

But he cannot remember his name. Jan Pelgrom sees the dead boy's face in his memory and longs to know where he is now. Is there a land after death? he thinks. A land more unknown than this one? And is the boy walking that land now with Wouter Loos? And Jan Pelgrom starts crying. He is suddenly overwhelmed with grief at not knowing the dead boy's name. And he wonders how long it will be until Wouter's name fades from him. And when he himself dies here, how long will anybody remember his own name?

'But it will not be me to blame,' he hisses into the unhearing ears of Wouter Loos. 'It was the devil! — *De Duivel!*'

And he recalls Jeronimus Cornelisz's terrible death vow from the gallows — a violent cry like the call of a thousand shrieking souls flying around the watchers' heads.

Terra Australis Incognita

Father Salvado stands on a small hill overlooking their mission huts. It has been a long slow trip back from Perth. But once again God has blessed him with His mercy, guided his hands, miraculously enabling him to raise the funds needed for supplies through singing the Lord's praise at a public concert.

He leads two oxen and a cart laden with food and tools. He had looked forward to the joy with which his brothers would greet his return. But his heart is heavy as he looks down on their small home. Four naked natives carry the body of Brother John Gorman. He has undergone a trial in the wilderness and lost. Some unknown darkness has reached out in the night and taken his life from them. The blacks are followed by the thin dark-robed figures of his brother Benedictines.

Suddenly Father Salvado can no longer see the dream of the tall stone church and monastery in this valley. And he knows that they will not be able to remain at this mission. He sees it suddenly for what it is. A small desolate hut touched and tainted by death.

Het Onbekende Zuidland

Jan Pelgrom is trying to describe a ship to the tribe. He must wait for the ship that will come and rescue him, he tells them. He tries to describe the tall masts and white sails. The creak of rope and timbers. The smell of paint and varnished wood. The cold heaviness of the cannons. But he has none of these words in their tongue.

So he tells them the story of the return of the commodore. He had sailed in a longboat from the shipwreck until he reached the Dutch East Indies. Then he returned on the ship *Sardam*.

The ship had appeared on the horizon one day, over 100 days after the shipwreck, and Jeronimus Cornelisz's evil world had fallen apart. Aghast, the Dutch sailors and soldiers had taken the devil and his men into captivity. Tortured them until word by word they revealed the whole story. They had murdered over 100 survivors of the shipwreck. One by one they named the dead, said the forbidden words.

And in the name of God, Commodore Pelsaert had chopped off the devil's hands and then he hanged him. *De Duivel*! And he had screamed and called down vengeance upon them all as they tightened the cord around his neck. A horrifying scream. And the sky went dark as the vengeful roar filled everyone's ears.

Then the commodore had hung all the mutineers. All except himself and Wouter Loos. He had spared them, and sent them to live with the tribe so that he, Jan Pelgrom, might tell them that story.

Terra Australis Incognita

'What has become of your dream?' asks Father Serra. He has been tending to Brother Fonteinne, who has been ill since they reached the site of their new mission on the banks of the Moore River.

'It is still strong,' says Father Salvado. 'With hard work and strength of faith we shall accomplish it.'

Once again their first task was to pray for their new mission home and begin constructing a hut. This time the natives assisted them. Eagerly following the black-robed men's instructions and examples. Listening patiently as they struggled with their language: *uango*, a hammer; *cattaculo*, to carry from one place to another; *dilagn*, something new that is just made.

Father Serra is weary and wishes to share Father Salvado's vision. 'Tell me about it again,' he says.

In two days the hut is finished and they are constructing an altar for services. The hut is far superior to their first home, but it is still far short of Father Salvado's tall stone church.

Father Salvado stares up at the heavens, letting the floating white clouds carry his thoughts a moment. 'We shall raise a monastery. And we shall name it Nova Nursia, after the birthplace of St Benedict,' he says. 'It will have tall stone buildings that can resist the dry heat and bushfires of this land. We shall graze sheep and cattle and raise crops that will help the monastery prosper. The natives will live at the monastery, learning the words of God, learning trades and earning their keep.'

'On this site?' asks Father Serra, turning and looking around at the dense bushland.

'Perhaps. Perhaps at another site. If this mission fails we will move to another. And another. We shall face each adversity as it confronts us and we shall overcome. We shall turn away plagues, floods and fires with our faith. We shall show the natives the strength of God is in our hands. And we shall win them to His word.'

Then he says, '*Motogon*', the native word for God.

Het Onbekende Zuidland

Jan Pelgrom is painting ships on the wall of a cave. He has been ill for several days. Finds the cool interior of the cave is easier to endure than the heat of the land. His tribal wife calls to him from outside. Tells him she has been looking for him. He says he will come soon. One of their children is ill, she tells him. They have been hunting, but have caught no game. He says he will come soon and resumes painting. Sits down and puts his head in his hands. Wonders if Wouter Loos felt this way in his last days.

He still dreams of the ship that will come for him. Still tells the story around the campfire at nights. Still tells how the ship came and overthrew the devil. Still tells the tribe how it will come for him one day and save him. With white sails like clouds. He feels it will come very soon.

Terra Australis Incognita

The natives have brought in a sick boy. He has a high fever and diarrhoea. Father Salvado does not know how to treat him. He asks the natives for the cause of the illness.

The natives say, '*Cienga*.' It is their word for the devil, he who causes all evil and harm in their lives. Brings storms, sends lightning down upon them, creeps around their camp at dark. Kills their children.

Father Salvado uses the only medicines he has to hand, olive oil and epsom salts and, while he tends to the boy, he tells the natives how God can vanquish the devil.

He quotes Christ overcoming the devil in the wilderness: '*Then saith Jesus unto him, get thee hence, Satan: for it is written, Thou shalt worship the Lord thy God and him only shall thou serve.*'

The natives beside him listen carefully. And then one old man nods his head repeatedly. As if he knows the story. '*De Duivel*,' he says.

Do You Remember When You Heard Kennedy Had Been Killed?

Cape York, 1848

Kennedy's blood is draining out of him. Seeping slowly into the damp soil. He is lying in the mud with three spear wounds: one in his back, one in his side and one in his thigh. He can feel his life slipping away. He knows he will never see civilisation again. Will probably never see another civilised person again. Will die in this accursed tropical wilderness.

The reporters crowd around him closely, eager to see every trickle of his blood. They can tell he hasn't got much time left. Can see the red flecks appearing in his spittle. It is tragic, they think. That is the word, tragic. The rescue ship *Ariel* barely ten miles away and Edmund Kennedy, after crossing hundreds of miles of wilderness, has been speared within reach of safety. They write in their open notebooks, Tragic.

'Would you describe your situation as tragic?' one of the reporters asks. A small fat man in a dark cardigan, coming undone at the sleeves.

Edmund Kennedy looks around himself, his eyes widening a little, and he opens his lips to speak. The reporters poise their pencils over their pads, ready to spear them down sharply, recording his dying words. But he says nothing.

'Mr Kennedy,' says another reporter, stepping a little closer. He is also a small man. With a bright red bulb of a nose. A map of purple veins. 'You've just been speared,' he says. 'Some would say you're dying.'

Edmund Kennedy blinks a little and turns to this man. The reporters ready their sharp pencils again. 'How does it feel?' the vein-nosed reporter asks. But Kennedy only stares at him as if he is speaking a foreign tongue that he cannot understand.

'They will call your expedition a failure,' says another reporter, also a small man. As he calls to the explorer his eyebrows rise like dark question marks.

Edmund Kennedy licks his pale lips. Slowly. Leaves blood on them. Wants to ask them, who exactly will call it a failure? But he cannot draw breath. The spear appears to have pierced his lungs.

'They will say you failed,' says the reporter again. 'Say that you never even completed half your expedition. Never even crossed to the gulf. They will say that your men died and that you let the empire down.'

Edmund Kennedy tries to shake his head. It has not been his fault. He has been a great man. A noble leader. He has struggled against untold adversities. Picking his way along a stretch of coast never meant to be trodden by men with carts and sheep. The marine surveyors, Captain Owen Stanley and Phillip Parker King, were both fools to believe that an overland journey to Port Essington should be made along the Cape and not further inland. And he was a fool to have agreed to lead the expedition on that route. A fool for fame and immortality. A damned fool.

'Damned!' he tries to mutter. But the words will not come. He looks again at the ring of reporters encircling him.

They have no idea of the difficulties of travelling through jungles and mangroves. Progressing inch by inch. Have no idea how the toil could wear men down. Even the greatest of men. He has to try to tell them.

'Would you call yourself a poor leader?' calls another reporter.

Now Kennedy tries to rise up on one elbow. He looks around for Jackey Jackey who has been carrying him for the past day. Carrying the weight of leadership of the expedition. He looks for him, but cannot see him, only the ring of wild men around him.

He waves an arm feebly, trying to ward them off. But they press closer. They know it won't be long now. They want the last words.

'Mr Kennedy,' calls the reporter with the dark cardigan. 'How did it feel when the men began dying on you?'

Kennedy remembers that the first death on the expedition was a native they had shot for attacking them. Then there was Mr Costigan. He wants to tell them that was an accident. The fool shot himself while struggling to get his rifle under cover, out of the drenching rain. And he wants to tell this to the reporters. Wants to tell them how it both saddened and angered him. And the rains, and the ticks, and leeches. And how the expedition livestock died, then their meat went putrid. They could only make two or three miles' progress each day. It was an impossible task. But he also wants to tell them that he never gave up. Never!

'Who would you blame for your failure?' calls another reporter.

'Yes, who?'

'Who?'

They are pushing closer now. Almost right on top of him. Frenzied. Close enough to reach out and touch him if they dared. Sharpened pencils poised menacingly. Then the small reporter in the dark cardigan leans a little closer and asks, 'Will you blame the blacks?'

The others watch cautiously. Wait to see what Mr Kennedy's response will be.

'The blacks have pursued you for days, have they not?' the small man asks. 'Have cast spears at your back in cowardly attacks. Have hidden in the shadows to ambush you. Robbed you when you were wounded. Slain your men.'

Edmund Kennedy looks about him fearfully. Where is Jackey Jackey? Have these wild men gotten to him already? Or has he escaped? Is he making his way to the ship with the expedition journals? He hopes to God he has escaped these savages.

The short fat reporter in the dark cardigan sees that Mr Kennedy is not able to answer him and swats a mosquito on his face. He looks at it distastefully. He is growing bored with this already. He lowers his pencil and picks at the wool around his frayed sleeve. Unravels it a little. Then he turns to regard the men around him.

'Personally,' he says, 'I think the colonies and the empire need great men like Mr Kennedy. And he could be a very great man. A great leader. He led his expedition through inhospitable lands where no white man had ever trodden before. But he was dealt a cruel blow by the treacherous natives.'

The men around him nod and make a note in their books. Treacherous natives.

The man standing directly beside the cardiganed reporter, an illustrator, begins drawing a quick sketch. A picture of Mr Kennedy standing, pitching forward, with a spear having struck him in the back. His arms are thrown up — the great man struck down by a cowardly attack. The pose is quite heroic, the reporter thinks, quite appropriate. The illustrator then draws some dark hidden faces peering around thick tree trunks — the savage assailants.

The reporter glances around cautiously. Just to make sure there aren't any dark faces there, hunting them, spears poised. But he sees nothing. There aren't even thick trees in the grassy plain where Edmund Kennedy lies dying. He swats at another mosquito.

The small man with the blood-veined nose leans forward and asks, 'Mr Kennedy, would you describe the blacks as treacherous?' He has already written the word but he wants to hear Mr Kennedy say it.

But Mr Kennedy says nothing. The reporter sees that he will have to prompt him a little. 'Fetch the black boy,' he says.

'Yes. Fetch the black boy,' says the dark-cardiganed reporter.

The ring of men opens a little and one of them pushes Jackey Jackey forward. The ring closes behind him and he falls to his knees by the dying explorer.

Edmund Kennedy recognises him at once. 'Jackey Jackey,' he says softly. The reporters stab their pencils to their pads as the two men talk.

'Are you well now?' asks Jackey Jackey.

'I don't care for the spear wound in my leg, Jackey, but for the other two spear wounds in my side and back, and I am bad inside, Jackey!'

The reporters listen, scribbling the words quickly. But Jackey Jackey replies so softly they can't quite hear and have to press closer.

Jackey Jackey has said that black fellows always die when they get speared in the back. Edmund Kennedy then coughs up a little pink spittle. The reporters wait for the words to come.

'I am out of wind, Jackey.'

'Are you going to leave me?'

'Yes, my boy; I am going to leave you; I am very bad, Jackey, you take the books, Jackey, to the Captain, but not the big ones; the Governor will give you anything for them.'

Jackey Jackey nods.

'Jackey, give me paper and I will write.'

The reporters press in even closer still, anxious to see what the great man will write.

Jackey Jackey draws out a piece of paper and a pencil from somewhere inside his clothes and passes them to the dying man, guiding his fingers around them. Mr Kennedy looks hard at them a moment, then slowly stabs the pencil to the paper. But before he can write a single word he falls back, dead.

The small man with the dark cardigan kicks Mr Kennedy in the leg. Then again, closer to the spear wound.

'He's definitely dead,' he says. 'A pity. That was getting quite good.'

'Do you think the black boy speaks English?' asks another reporter, despite having just written down Jackey Jackey's conversation with Mr Kennedy.

'Probably not very well,' says the vein-nosed reporter.

'Ask him,' says the reporter in the dark cardigan, picking at the thread around his sleeve once more.

'You speekee English?' asks the vein-nosed reporter.

Jackey Jackey lifts his head slowly and looks at him. He regards the curious markings on the man's nose. Like a map of the rivers of the Cape country around them. He regards all the reporters carefully. Knows that, like the Yadhaigana people, through whose land they are passing, these men are waiting for a chance for confrontation, and will turn violent if provoked by the wrong actions. He knows he should not take his eyes from them. Knows how suddenly they could turn on him.

'You savvy?' the vein-nosed reporter asks again.

Jackey Jackey nods his head slowly. 'I speak good English,' he says.

The reporters all smile as one. Like a pack. 'What's your name?' asks the reporter in the dark cardigan, very slowly.

'They call me Jackey Jackey,' he says. He has no intention of telling them his real name — Galmarra, the song man.

'You could be a hero if you're willing to cooperate with us,' says the cardiganed reporter.

Jackey Jackey narrows his eyes a little. 'What do you want?' he asks.

'We only want you to tell us what happened,' says the cardiganed reporter. 'We only want your story.'

Galmarra does not want to give these men his story. Knows they will take it and make it their own story.

'What do you want?' he asks again.

'How does this sound?' asks the vein-nosed reporter. 'Jackey Jackey is the finest type of noble savage, who alone lived to tell the tragic tale of the death of Mr Kennedy, who, so close to his goal, with treacherous natives persistently hanging on his footsteps, fell at last beneath their spears.'

'Yes, that's good,' says the dark-cardiganed man. 'But how will Jackey Jackey get away from the wild blacks?'

The reporters look at each other blankly. Then turn to Jackey Jackey. He looks back at them, and then says,

'That night I left him near dark. I would go through the scrub and the blacks threw spears at me; a great many; and I went back into the scrub. Then I went down the creek which runs into Escape River, and I walked along the water in the creek, very easy, with my head only above water, to avoid the blacks, and get out of their way. In this way I went half-a-mile. Then I got out of the creek and got clear

of them, and walked all night nearly, and slept in the bush without a fire.'

'Yes,' says the cardiganed man. 'Then he appears on the beach and waves wildly to the ship.'

'But they think he is one of the wild blacks,' says another, writing furiously in his book.

'Yes. But the savages are after him. They are onto his track. And if he cannot attract the attention of the crew they will spear him.'

'I like it,' says the reporter with the dark cardigan. 'It's got real drama. But he fails to attract their attention, until finally a boat comes to save him just as the wild blacks are about to cast spears into his back.'

'Only the heroic and devoted Jackey Jackey lived to tell the tale,' says the dark-cardiganed reporter again.

All the reporters write that line.

'And what about the rest of the party?' asks the vein-nosed reporter. 'The ones left behind at Shelburne Bay and at Weymouth Bay?'

The reporter with the dark cardigan picks distractedly at his sleeve again. Unravels the wool. Unravels the plot. 'I think we should let them die in the wild. Heroic but tragic deaths.'

'Perhaps we should save some?' says a man beside him. Younger than the rest, new at the trade. 'Jackey Jackey could lead a rescue party to save them just as the encircling blacks were about to spear them,' he says.

'Or perhaps they should all be slain and eaten by the blacks,' says the illustrator, planning the picture in his head already.

'Are they known to be cannibals?' the young reporter asks.

The rest of his colleagues turn to regard him with a scornful look. 'They will be if we report they are,' says the cardiganed reporter, as if stating one of the basic commandments.

'And what of Jackey Jackey?' asks the young reporter.

But the cardiganed man does not need to answer. Most of the reporters have known his type before, have interviewed him, have written his story. Made him into a hero. Rewarded him with valuables and attention. Maybe they'd even have an official lithograph of him made. Then one day he'd be left alone in the wilderness. Ignored as they moved onto the next story. He'd probably take to drink, end badly. Fall into a campfire or something.

'We'll make sure you're well provided for,' says the cardiganed reporter to Jackey Jackey. 'As long as you cooperate with us.'

'First I bury Mr Kennedy,' says Jackey Jackey.

'It doesn't matter,' says the cardiganed reporter. 'As long as we say you've buried him, he will be buried.' He slaps at another mosquito. Wants to be gone from this infernal damp swamp.

'How does this sound?' he asks. 'You say,

I caught him in my arms and held him; and then I turned round myself and cried. I was crying a good while until I got well; that was about an hour, and then I buried him. I digged up the ground with a tomahawk, and covered him over with logs and grass and my shirt and trousers. That night I left him near dark.'

'It sounds fine to me,' says another reporter, also writing it down. Also wishing to be gone from there.

'Truly the noblest of noble savages,' says the vein-nosed reporter. And then, quite overcome by his own purple prose, says, 'In the cities this story will be the sensation of the year. People will weep when they read our reports. They will raise a public subscription to fund the building of a cenotaph on this site, larger than that built for fallen warriors. And they will look back, many years hence, and ask each other if they remembered what they were doing when they heard the news that Mr Kennedy had been killed.'

The other reporters nod, make more notes, slap at mosquitoes.

'Fine, then,' says the dark-cardiganed reporter, still unravelling his sleeve further. 'I think we can finish up here.' Then he says to Jackey Jackey, 'You can carry our gear.'

'I carry Mr Kennedy's journals to safety,' says Jackey Jackey. 'I save Mr Kennedy's story.'

'The journals!' says the reporter with the dark cardigan. 'Yes. The journals! We've got to have those.' The reporters all turn towards the explorer's saddle bags. The journals might only have the scantest of lines in them, but they will tell Mr Kennedy's story in his own words. Much more tragic than the black boy's words. They can take his words of grief and suffering and self-doubt and accusations of official incompetence and turn him into a valiant hero. Yes. They must have them!

They quickly pick through the saddle bags. But they are empty! The reporters turn back to Jackey Jackey, anger on their faces. But he is gone.

'The little devil,' says the reporter with the veined nose. 'Quick. After him. We've got to get those journals before he reaches the ship.'

But Jackey Jackey is gone. Melted into the darkness. Wading the crocodile-infested rivers with only his head out of the water. Carrying the heavy burden of Mr Kennedy's story to safety. He will never deliver the journals to the captain of the *Ariel*. He arrives with only a small notebook and his own story. But he will carry the weight of that story forever.

The Three Gospels of the Reverend Lancelot Threlkeld

Lake Macquarie, 1859

Gospel 1

'In the beginning was the Word and the Word was with God.'
John 1:1

The Reverend Lancelot Threlkeld tries to recall how it was said in the Awabakal language. He sits in his small dim study, carefully going over his manuscript of Luke's gospel. The many years of toil he has devoted to it have left the pages a little stained and frayed. He reads the last line of Luke aloud: *'Gatun kakilliela murrug hieron ka, murrarag wiyelliela gatun pitamulliela bon Eloinug.'*

He enunciates the words carefully, but wonders if he has gotten the tone just right. He wishes his assistant, McGill, was still with him to help him. To guide him through the pronunciation. To read the words aloud for him just one more time.

He wishes any of the Awabakal people were still alive to read his gospel. He reads the last line out in English: *'And were continually in the temple, praising and blessing God.'*

He closes the last page of the manuscript and rests his head upon it. His life's work. Eighteen years of toil. He had devoted his life to working with the Awabakal people, giving them the lord's word in their own tongue, and now it is only a curiosity.

Gatun kakilliela murrug hieron ka, murrarag wiyelliela gatun pitamulliela bon Eloinug.

Gospel 2

McGill always left quite an impression on the Europeans who met him. His command of English was good, his bearing was noble, and his understanding of European foibles and prejudices was acute.

'How remarkable,' many would comment. 'Quite an accomplishment,' some would say. And they would congratulate the Reverend Threlkeld, as if McGill's intelligence were of his personal doing.

But McGill knew who was the teacher and who was the student. He led the Reverend Threlkeld around his land and through his language and customs, carefully sounding out the words. Repeating them over and over while the Reverend Threlkeld wrestled with the sounds.

He told McGill many times that he must learn their language before he could preach to them. 'The Awabakal people are like an untilled field,' he would say, while instructing them in the process of ploughing the soil at the Bahtahbah mission station. 'And as a farmer needs his tools, a missionary needs the gospels.'

McGill translated the Reverend Threlkeld's words and instructions to his people and they watched carefully as the soil was turned. 'Tomorrow we shall sow the seeds,' the Reverend Threlkeld explained.

But the next day they went hunting.

Gospel 3

The Reverend Lancelot Threlkeld had an ambitious dream for Bahtahbah mission, a dream of a cleared path that ran through the wild bushland around Lake Macquarie and led to the cultivated land of the mission, to sanctuary. A village where the Aborigines lived in well-built huts and worshipped the Lord in their own language.

On some nights that path was so clear before him that he could almost step out and walk it.

The soil was hard and the climate harsh, but he would persevere. His dream was strong. He could see a church building, schools and huts. He could see cleared fields full of crops. *'Self-sufficiency'*, he had promised the London Mission Society directors. He would grow a sanctuary for the gospels and Christian enlightenment amongst a hostile landscape.

'*I wish to make known Salvation to the aborigines in their own tongue,*' he had promised the Reverend Samuel Marsden, who oversaw his finances. And he had dreamt of the day when he himself could preach those gospels to them.

Gospel 1

The Reverend Threlkeld sits at his desk and turns over a new page. It seems he is spending more time each day on correspondence and less time with his gospels. But he needs to defend himself, needs to obtain funding for his work. He writes:

> *My own attempt in favour of the aborigines of New South Wales was commenced in the year 1824, under the auspices of the London Missionary Society, at the request of the deputation from that Institution sent out for the purpose of establishing a Mission in the East, and urged likewise by the solicitations of the local Government of this colony. The British Government sanctioned the project by authorizing a grant of 10,000 acres of land at Lake Macquarie, in trust for the said purpose, at the recommendation of Sir Thomas Brisbane, the Governor of the Australian Colonies.*
>
> *In 1839, the London Missionary Society abandoned the mission, broke faith with me, and left me to seek such resources as the providence of God might provide, after fifteen years' service in their employ.*

His hand still shakes to defend himself.

Gospel 2

McGill watched the Reverend Lancelot Threlkeld struggling for words. The congregation sat before him, patiently, as he picked his way through the Awabakal words, trying to bring some of his passion to their meaning. But they looked back with silent dark faces.

The Reverend Threlkeld clenched his hands, turned and sat down. Pushed his fists into his eyes.

McGill, always beside him, placed one hand on his shoulder and asked him, 'What do you wish to tell them?'

'I wish to comfort them for their loss,' he said. 'I wish to tell them the Lord's words:

Blessed are they that mourn: for they shall be comforted. Blessed are they which do hunger and thirst after righteousness: for they shall be filled. Blessed are ye, when men shall revile you, and persecute you, and shall say all manner of evil against you falsely, for my sake.

'Then we are truly blessed,' said McGill and turned back towards the altar.

Gospel 3

The Reverend Threlkeld has a dark dream. He has almost completed translating the whole Bible into Awabakal. He has reached the final book — the Revelation of St John the Divine. The dreams and nightmare visions of St John. '*And I looked and beheld a pale horse; and his name that sat on him was Death, and Hell followed with him.*'

And as he puts down the words he sees the pale rider before him, on a tall white horse. Death in his hands. Guns and long knives. '*And power was given unto them, to kill with sword, and with hunger, and with death ...*' And the Reverend Threlkeld sees the pale rider ride into the mission, and he points at the Awabakal people. Singling them out.

The Reverend Threlkeld wants to call out to the people, to warn them. But he cannot. As he reaches for the Awabakal words they fade from his mind.

Gospel 1

The Reverend Threlkeld sits in his study and writes:

This year a party of Blacks consisting of almost 26 were at work at a station, the overseer told them to go away as the stockmen were out after the Blacks to punish them, they did not go, the stockmen came, ripped open the bellies of the blacks, killed the women, took the children by the legs and dashed their brains out against the trees. They then made a triangle log fire to burn the bodies, and reserved two little girls about 7 years old for Lascivious purposes and because they were too small for them they cut them with knives.

His hands quiver as he writes. But he persists:

Mr Day also informed me of the number said to be slain 500 including Major Nunn's slaughter, and from various others I heard the same as a common report — the Revd Mr Wilton mentioned the number also to me, likewise Mr Cobb, where Major Nunn made his boast before a large party of 'Popping off with his holster pistols the Blacks whenever one appeared from behind a tree'.

Gospel 2

McGill brings the young man Davey into the Reverend Threlkeld's study. 'I have brought him,' he says.

The Reverend Threlkeld tries to appear as if he is busy, working on his manuscript, but McGill will not leave. Finally the Reverend Threlkeld turns and addresses them. 'Very well lad, tell me what you saw.'

The young man's English is quite good. He uses the words well. He tells the Reverend Threlkeld everything. Tells him that he saw the white men ride into their camp and begin shooting and stabbing. He tells him in graphic detail how one elderly woman's throat was cut as she stood there and then tried to run, with the blood spurting freely. He tells how the white men chased her, and took her, while still alive yet and threw her onto a triangular log fire. Then they cast an infant onto the fire with her.

As he tells the story his eyes fill with the memory of it, and he mimics the sounds of the dying and the cries of the wounded.

'How many were slain?' the Reverend Threlkeld asks, with his eyes shut. But he doesn't hear the answer. He only hears the wails of the dying and wounded.

Gospel 3

There are rumours of another massacre wafting around the lake's edge. Whispered words of dead bodies, shot and hacked and left for the crows to pick over. There is a faint stench of burnt flesh seeping around the lake's shore.

The Reverend Lancelot Threlkeld tries to hide from them. Tries to block out the words, block out the stench. But it is unrelenting. It creeps under his door and seeps into his conscience. He tries to concentrate on his work, his translation of the holy scriptures. That is his task.

But he knows that they are Awabakal eyes that now lie lifeless in the gorges and the marshes, and will never read his work.

Gospel 1

The Reverend Threlkeld is in his study working on his gospel. He is immersed in the death of Christ. He prints the words carefully, marking in the accents to show the correct pronunciation:

Wonto buru ba wiyá, wiyelliela, Buwa bon tetti, buwa bon tetti.
Gatun noa barun wiya yukita garo-ka, Minarig tin?
Minarig noa yarakai uma? Keawai bag gurrapa taraikan gikoug kin galoa kolag búnkilli kolag tetti wissilliko; wélkorinun wal ban bag, gaun wamunbinun bon.
Gatun bara tanoa-kal-bo pullí kakulla kauwal wiyelliela, búwil koa bon tetti-gatun pulli borúnba gatun barúnba piriwal hierou pirral kakulla.
Gatun Pilatorto noa wiyá, ka-uwil koa yanti wiya bara bo.

Then he repeats the words in his own tongue:

But they cried, saying, Crucify him, crucify him.
And he said unto them the third time, Why, what evil hath he done? I have found no cause of death in him: I will therefore chastise him, and let him go.
And they were insistent with loud voices, requiring that he might be crucified. And the voices of them and of the chief priests prevailed.
And Pilate gave sentence that it should be as they required.

Gospel 2

McGill brought the old man to the Reverend Threlkeld, and they have been talking together. He is one of the few Awabakal elders still alive. The reverend has had difficulty following the words. He understands 'death' and 'crucifix' and asks McGill if the man is telling him a gospel story of Christ.

But McGill says no, he is telling the story of a black man who lived near Moreton Bay. A man named Dundalli. He was big trouble for the troopers there, he says. He rallied the blacks together. He speared cattle or attacked white men, then he travelled at night and reappeared to attack the settlers where they weren't expecting him. He fought for his land and his people.

'But they caught him and killed him,' he says. Hung him on a crucifix. One of his own betrayed him. Then they hung him. Strung him up by the neck, with his arms stretched out wide.

'But he didn't die,' says McGill. Not straight away. He was too big for them. He grew and grew until his feet touched the ground. And he called out to his people there to save him, to avenge him. Said he would return and save them.

The soldiers had to lift his feet up. Stab him in the side with a sword. Then they left him there for three days until he was good and dead.

'That's how they killed him,' says McGill.

Gospel 3

The Reverend Lancelot Threlkeld lies alone, staring out at the darkness of the night. He is certain he can hear the distant footfall of heavy boots outside. He is sure he can hear the clink of metal upon metal. He recognises the distant snort of horses. He knows they are coming for him. A large group of them, guns ready, on pale horses.

They will surround him silently in the darkness. Patiently taking up their positions, awaiting the first hint of morning. Then they will ride hard across the landscape, horse hooves drumming rapidly. They will come from all sides, converging upon him. Guns blazing. Firing slanders and accusations. He will turn to face them. Staring contemptuously at his attackers. But they will overwhelm him. Drive him from the mission. Leave him lying in a ditch somewhere for the crows to pick over.

Gospel 1

The Reverend Lancelot Threlkeld hungers and thirsts for justice's sake. His salary has been stopped by the governor and he has been officially requested to leave the mission. He has written to the governor requesting funding to work with the few Awabakal people who have moved towards Newcastle, where they are being attacked by rum and prostitution and European diseases. He has argued that they will still have need of his gospels.

But even that is refused him.

The Reverend Threlkeld writes:

In submitting to this decision it is impossible not to feel considerable disappointment to the expectations formerly hoped to be realised in the conversion of some, at least, of the Aborigines in this part of the colony, and not to express concern that so many years of constant attention appear to have been fruitlessly expended. It is, however, perfectly apparent that the termination of the Mission has arisen solely from the Aborigines becoming extinct in these districts and the very few that remain elsewhere are so scattered ... The thousands of Aborigines ... decreased to hundreds, the hundreds have lessened to tens, and the tens will dwindle into units, before a very few years shall have passed away.

Gospel 2

McGill comes into the Reverend Threlkeld's study. Waits patiently and then tells him there have been more murders. Not by the soldiers this time. By convict labourers. They have killed a large group of Weraerai people. Chopped the bodies up. Burnt some. Made no attempt to hide them. They left their bones hanging on crude crosses for the magpies to pick over.

'Where did this happen?' asks the Reverend Threlkeld, feeling suddenly very weary. Fearful of how much closer to his mission this latest massacre may have occurred.

'They call it Myall Creek,' says McGill.

The Reverend Threlkeld closes his eyes.

Gospel 3

The Reverend Threlkeld pulls his blanket high over his head and tries to concentrate on his prayers. But there is a distant cry outside in the night. A long and fearful wailing. Maybe it is just an animal, he thinks. Maybe he is imagining it, he hopes. Maybe it will be gone by morning, he prays.

But it is louder and clearer than he has ever heard it before. Close enough to creep under his door and linger in the dark corners of his chamber. And he wonders if the voices are calling on him to save them. To avenge them.

Gospel 1

The Reverend Threlkeld stands in his small mission church and reads to the dwindling congregation gathered there, in their own language:

Keawai noa unti, kulla noa waita ka ba bougkullún:
gurrulla nura yanti wiya nurun noa ba, yakita noa ba
kakulla Galilaia ka,
Wiyelliela, Yinal to kuri koba wunun wal bon mattara yara
kai — willug koba ka, gatun búnnun wal tetti, gatun
purreagka tarai ka kúmbaken bougkullîa kanun noa.
Gatun gaiya bara kotelliela gikoúmba wiyelli tara.

Then he repeats the words in his own tongue:

He is not here, but is risen: remember how he spake unto
you when he was yet in Galilee
Saying, The Son of man must be delivered into the hands of
sinful men, and be crucified, and the third day rise again.
And they remembered his words.

Gospel 2

McGill tells the Reverend Threlkeld about Dundalli's resurrection.

'The soldiers were unable to kill him,' he says. They tried to crucify him on the gallows. But he was too clever for them. The story says that he came back to life. Rose up and walked the land again. And he was even more powerful this time. They would never be able to kill him again. 'And he was going to save his people,' McGill says. He was going to lead them in their fight against their oppressors.

The Reverend Threlkeld shakes his head slowly. 'But this is amazing,' he says. 'Where did that man say he heard this story from?'

'He says he heard it from you,' says McGill.

Gospel 3

The Reverend Lancelot Threlkeld looks out into the darkness. The governor, the Reverend Samuel Marsden and the London Missionary Society have come to his mission in the night and seized him while he was at prayer and have dragged him deep into the bushland.

It is dark and black where they have taken him. The only light is from a small fire. A fire of dark limbs and corpses. The flames throw up a dancing light upon a scaffold. A crucifix. And several convict labourers seize him. Push him to the ground. Strip him of his garments and then retire to the fireside to gamble for them.

Then the New South Wales military, led by Major Nunn, are upon him. They kick him in the chest. They rub his face into the dirt, standing on his head with their heavy boots. They hold him down while the directors of the London Missionary Society approach him. And they scourge him with their tongues. Accuse him of mismanagement, of corruption, of excesses. He tries to protest his innocence, but the words will not come.

Then, when they are finally done, they take him and cast him upon the crucifix. They fix him there with cruel hands and leave him there for the first light. For all the people of the colony to see.

Gospel 1
The Reverend Threlkeld sits with his translation of Luke's gospel. He is writing an introduction to it in English, so that there will be something of it that can be read.

> *Under such circumstances, the translation of the Gospels by St Luke can only be now a work of curiosity — a record of the language of a tribe that once existed, and would have, otherwise been numbered with those nations and their forgotten languages, and people with their unknown tongues, who have passed away from this globe and are buried in oblivion.*

Gospel 2
McGill sits by the Reverend Threlkeld's side. Helping him write the words of God. The Reverend Threlkeld repeats them over and over until he is sure they have it just right. Then he commits the words to paper.

They have been working like this for many years and have now reached the last line of Luke's gospel. The Reverend Threlkeld prints the words carefully then reads the last line back to McGill: '*Gatun kakilliela murrug hieron ka, murrarag wiyelliela gatun pitamulliela bon Eloinug.*'

McGill smiles and nods his head. The Reverend Threlkeld feels immensely filled, immensely comforted.

'Thank you McGill,' he says. And he suddenly recalls that McGill has another name, his tribal name. 'Biraban,' he says.

But he does not reply.

Gospel 3
The Reverend Threlkeld sits with his manuscript of Luke's gospel. He has brushed the dust off the manuscript and written an introduction for it. He and McGill had begun work on Mark's Gospel and he had some dreams for John as well. But they were

beyond his reach now. There would only ever be Luke's words in Awabakal. And only himself to read them.

He looks at the words before him and is no longer certain about them. He is trying to remember the declensions of the verb 'to die'. He could once write out ten different declensions without pause. But now he has to struggle for them.

He says aloud, '*Tetti bulliko*, which means to be in the act of dying'. That's the first one.

Then, '*Tetti ba-uwil-koa noa*, in order that he might die. And *Tetti béa-kun-koa noa*, lest he should die.'

He pauses and thinks. Has to reach far out into the past to find the words. '*Tetti bá-non noa ba*, if he should die. *Tetti bá-ga noa*, he had almost died. *Tetti ba-pa noa*, if he died.'

Then there is blankness. He closes his eyes and grasps around in the darkness. *Tetti ba*-something was to proceed to die. And then … and then … to die again. What were the words to die again?

Perhaps if he reads his text it will come to him. He turns to the beginning once more. Places one finger on the first line of Luke. Begins reading it all over again: '*Wonto ba kauwallo mankulla unnoa tara túgunbilli ko gurrántogéen kinba.*'

Dig: The Forgotten History of Burke and Wills

Central Australia, 1861

Robert O'Hara takes off his top hat and bends slowly down once more to taste the brackish knee-deep water.

'It's definitely salty now,' he says. 'Taste it yourself.'

John Wills holds himself against a mangrove tree and leans forward a little. He carefully sniffs the water. It smells of mud and rotting things that fill his head and make him dizzy.

'Taste it,' says Robert O'Hara. 'It's salty.'

Wills just shrugs a little. Then nods. He hasn't any strength left to argue.

Robert O'Hara takes another drink. A larger one. 'We must be at the ocean now,' he says. 'Listen. Can you hear it?'

John Wills stares at the impenetrable barrier of mangroves before them. He closes his eyes. He can hear the gentle lap of water around their legs. He hears the buzzing of flies and mosquitoes. He hears a slight wind in the leaves. And he hears their own laboured breathing.

He opens his eyes again and stares once more at the mangroves. They go on forever.

'Yes, I believe I can hear it too,' he says. 'I think we can turn back now.'

At the edge of the desert, on their slow trek northwards, Wills had found fossil sea shells.

'What does it mean?' asked Mr Gray, the sailor. 'Does it mean that we've reached the sea?' But around them, as far as he could see, was an ocean of desert.

'Yes, perhaps we have,' said John Wills, forever making maps in his head, redrawing an ancient ocean across the top of the continent. 'But we are about one million years too late.'

Mr Gray didn't understand what he meant. But he knew he could smell moisture in the air. 'The ocean is near,' he said.

Wills shook his head, and then looked up as the heavy clouds above them opened up and a downpour like the sea falling on them assailed the four men.

It rains for 40 days and 40 nights as they crossed into the tropics. The camels began to weigh upon them like a great burden. Their large twin-toed feet bog down constantly in the ocean of mud. The beasts refuse to rise each morning, and they refuse to kneel down after each long day's walking. They stop for no reason, slowly sinking in the mud. They snort and grunt when the explorers pull frustratedly on their nose pegs, attempting to get them to move.

The men say, 'Moosh, moosh,' and 'Hooshta,' just like the Indian cameleers did. But they can't make it sound quite right.

Robert O'Hara had dismissed the cameleers along with the native guides. He has pegged his faith on the supremacy of British technology. Compass and sextants and pistols and sturdy British boots.

Robert O'Hara urged the other three men in the advance party to press on. He reassured them that when they found flat dry ground again the camels slow ambling gait would carry them onwards forever. Then they'd eat up the miles. But silently, in his own inner rage, Robert O'Hara considered shooting the beasts and being done with them.

Once, in anger, when the lead camel refused to rise one morning, he pulled out his revolver and aimed it squarely at the animal's head.

Mr King said, 'That one's carrying the water!'

Robert O'Hara lowered his revolver and stared at the beast in distaste. 'Is this one of the camels brought from India?' he asks.

'No sir,' says King, 'That is one of those we procured from the Melbourne opera company.'

'Then it should be no surprise that it is more used to tragedy than travel,' says John Wills.

Robert O'Hara narrows his eyes and stares at the camel distrustfully. Has this beast been close to his own beloved Julia Matthews on some dim theatre stage? She is a secret the men know nothing about. He snorts and grunts, then he spits at the beast and walks away.

'We never had camels in the Hussars,' he grumbles.

Each morning Robert O'Hara asks John Wills to map out for him their progress and anticipated day's journey. Wills adds to the maps in his head every day. The last thing Robert O'Hara asks him is which direction they will head in that day. That is another secret of his. He cannot tell, one day to the next, where they have come from and where they are going.

As they trek northwards towards the ocean they cross innumerable small creeks, fed by the heavy rains running off the hills around them. Robert O'Hara has taken upon himself the burden of naming each one. He has named the whole area Cloncurry, after a well-to-do family from County Galway, and has now depleted the names of his family and kin and all the near and far neighbours from Ireland. And still they encounter more creeks.

He knows the men with him are expectant that they too might have some landmark named after them. But Robert O'Hara does not give out immortality easily.

Finally towards evening, they cross three small creeks, created by the rain, each no larger than a single pace across. The camels don't even appear to see them. John Wills walks up to Robert O'Hara's side and although he has never asked a favour of his commander, he says, 'Sir?'

Robert O'Hara tries to look absorbed in studying the horizon, but he is trying, in fact, to recall the names of the three children who sat in front of his desk in his first year of school. The thought of being forgotten like that sends a chill through him.

'Oh blast it all,' he says. 'All right, King Creek, Grey Creek and Wills Creek!'

Finally even John Wills admits they are lost. So close to the gulf, but trapped between rocky cliffs and gullies that block their way, forcing them to turn back on their own tracks. Time and time again. The heat seems to be melting the fine details of Wills's mental maps.

Then they encounter the blacks.

Robert O'Hara keeps his hand on his pistol, while John Wills and Mr King try and talk to them. They wave their hands and scratch in the earth. Wills comes back excitedly. 'They have shown us the way to the plains,' he says. 'And they wish for us to join them in a meal.'

Mr Grey, the sailor, smiles broadly.

Robert O'Hara is distrustful. But he nods assent.

'And there is something else,' says Mr King, his youthful embarrassment showing. 'They have offered us their women.'

Mr Grey is still smiling.

But Robert O'Hara turns dark and solemn. 'Thank them for the directions only,' he says. 'We will leave at once. We cannot afford to lose our way this close to our goal.'

At nights they sit around the campfire and Robert O'Hara delights them with tales of his life as a Hussar and accounts of his years spent in the Hapsburgs' court in Vienna. He tells them of the duel that earned him a deep scar under his beard. He tells them of the glitter and grandeur of it all. He tells them of the campaigns and battles he's been in. He tells them of his full life of adventure.

But there are other stories he doesn't tell them. Secret stories of his lusting thirst for fame. How disappointing he'd found life in the Hussars with no wars to fight. No glory to win. How he returned to Ireland and joined the constabulary and that his first taste of battle was against his own people. Putting down the uprisings. Violently and shamefully attacking peasants and farmers of his neighbourhood who spoke his own tongue.

But then the newspapers were filled with tales of adventure and fortune to be won on the New South Wales goldfields. And he knew he could see his own name written there. And so he went.

He does not tell them how bitter it was to arrive at the Australian goldfields and find just how hard it was to make a fortune. And then to hear that his own brother had gone to the Crimea and had fallen in the campaign. The first officer to die! A glorious wonderful death. The newspapers were full of it.

Robert O'Hara left the colony at once and headed straight back to Europe, arriving just as the Crimean campaign ended. So he returned to Australia once more, bitter and angry. He took up a job as a policeman, working in a small rural town. Waiting for destiny to find him.

But he was pretty well hidden.

And then finally he saw the path before him. He read of the offer to lead the first party across the continent. He recognised it at once. That was a path to glory and fame, and it had his name written all over it. ROBERT O'HARA BURKE. In capital letters!

They were getting close now. Wills said the stream in front of them appeared to be tidal. Robert O'Hara then ordered Gray and King to remain behind while he and Mr Wills pushed on to the gulf. Both men tried to hide their disappointment but obeyed their leader. Standing to attention as he proceeded onwards.

Robert O'Hara plunged into the creek, thinking to himself, I will name this creek Julia Matthews Creek after my beloved, who is also tidal in her nature.

He will not look at the other two men as he proclaims this to himself, least his face should betray his emotions. Neither does he look at them as he wades through its warm waters and feels its flow softly licking at his privates.

King and Gray were waiting patiently where they had left them. Still at attention.

'Did you see the sea Mr Burke?' asks Gray, with a great longing to see the cool blueness again himself.

'Yes,' said Robert O'Hara.

'Tell me what it was like,' said Mr Gray. 'Please tell me what it looked like.'

'The waves sounded like the roar of distant cannon fire,' said Robert O'Hara.

They are soon back at the edge of the desert. Mr Gray is lying on the ground, his legs folded under him. Like a camel, Robert O'Hara thinks.

'Come on man, get up,' he says, a little louder this time. He adjusts his top hat. 'Think of all the people counting on you.'

But Gray says nothing.

'I am ordering you to your feet,' says Robert O'Hara. 'I am the leader of this expedition. And this is a direct order.'

But still Gray says nothing.

'This is insolence,' Robert O'Hara screams. 'Insolence and mutiny.' He looks around for his pistol, determined to teach the man a lesson.

John Wills comes up beside them. He looks carefully at Gray. 'He is dead,' he says.

Robert O'Hara looks at him a moment, and then at Mr Gray.

'Are you sure?' he asks.

John Wills bends down and touches the dead man's eyelids lightly with his fingers. Feels the chillness of death on him.

'Quite sure,' he says.

Robert O'Hara looks at John Wills. 'How awkward,' he says. 'I think we'd best bury him then.'

'The ground is very hard and rocky,' says John Wills.

'A Christian burial,' says Robert O'Hara, determinedly.

'Of course,' says John Wills and sets his watch to mark the task. He and King dig on the floor of the ancient ocean until their fingernails bleed.

'Nine hours,' mutters John Wills, as they put the last of the stones on top of their comrade's body, burying the lost day's travel with the corpse.

Back at Coopers Creek, hundreds of miles to the south, Mr Brahe, the Swede, has finished building the stockade, as per Mr Burke's last orders. The men were very diligent and the fortifications will withstand the charge of many hundred blacks.

Mr Brahe is quite aware that the blacks here about are very friendly, but it had been Mr Burke's orders, and he is always one to follow orders.

He now spends each day looking out at the distant northern horizon. Mr Burke's advance party is overdue. They only had three months' supplies with them. There is nobody left to give him orders. He is not sure what to do. Each day the men ask if they should load up the camels and depart. And each day he does not know what to tell them.

He sits on the hot sand and looks northwards. Sees the party emerging from the distance. The four men and the camels. Shimmering out there in the heat. He climbs to his feet as they dissolve back into the empty landscape.

He sees it every day. Over and over. Until he grows to distrust his own judgement.

It seems quieter at nights with just the three of them now.

'Tell us a story Mr King,' Robert O'Hara commands.

Young Mr King, ever eager to please, tells the men about his first military posting in India. He tells them the gory horrors of the mutiny, of how white men were cut up into tiny pieces, their blood spilled heavily into the earth.

He tells them of surprise attacks on white homesteads, on military camps or on lone travellers. How the natives would leap silently out of the night and run long sharp swords deep into men and women, howling for their blood.

'Thank you Mr King,' says Robert O'Hara, moving a little closer to the fire, 'That will be enough for this evening.'

The camels are not making good progress. They walk as if their legs are still bogged in the mud. Stumbling forward slowly. Refusing to rise in the mornings. Refusing to lie down in the evening.

'Hooshta, hooshta,' says Mr King vainly, his own feet stumbling.

Robert O'Hara fingers his pistol.

Finally the three men reach the fortified stockade at Coopers Creek. All done in. Barely able to drag their shadows after them.

Robert O'Hara looks around for Mr Brahe and the men. They are not there.

'Mr Brahe,' he calls, unable to comprehend the silence.

'The ashes of the fire are still warm, sir,' says King.

'That was very kind of them,' says Robert O'Hara. 'It has been getting very cold of evenings.'

John Wills then indicates the large coolibah tree with the word 'DIG' etched deeply into its bark. Still bleeding sap.

'Well we'd best dig then,' says Robert O'Hara, and settles back, adjusting his top hat, while Wills and King dig. They dig, again, until their fingernails bleed.

About three feet down they uncover a cache of food and a bottle. Wills holds it up.

'Splendid,' says Robert O'Hara. 'Let's breach it.'

John Wills unstops the bottle and looks in. 'It's a note,' he says, a little disappointed.

'Read it,' commands Robert O'Hara.

Mr Wills reads:

Depot Cooper's Creek. 21st April, 1861. The Depot Party of Victorian Exploring Expedition leaves this camp today to return to the Darling ... No person has been up here from the Darling. We have six camels and twelve horses in good working order. William Brahe.

John Wills stares at Robert O'Hara Burke, then looks out beyond the stockade walls and says, 'They're out there. Only nine hours away. Not much more than ten miles distant.'

The three men turn and look to the horizon, shading their eyes, trying to discern any movement. But their comrades might as well have been 100 miles away. Might as well have been a million years distant.

'They've forgotten us!' says Robert O'Hara in despair.

Two days later Robert O'Hara Burke awakens with a vision. He calls Mr King and Mr Wills to him.

'I have seen our salvation,' he says. And he points out across the desert in a more southwesterly direction. 'We will walk to South Australia, where Stuart would have gone. We will walk to the settlements there and be saved. They will carry us the rest of the way to Adelaide on their shoulders. Then on to Melbourne. We will be heroes.'

King nods eagerly. 'Yes, sir,' he says. 'We can do it.'

'What settlement should we aim to reach?' asks John Wills, still charting maps in his head.

'Mount Hopeless,' says Robert O'Hara. Then he points to the distance. 'I know it's late,' he says, 'But if we set off now we should be well up the creek by nightfall.'

After they have left the Coopers Creek camp for the final walk, King's shoes fall apart. He curses silently. Eighty pairs of boots they had packed, and not a single pair left to be had. He flings the scraps of leather far from him. Walks barefoot. The hot sharp earth tortures his feet. But only for a while. Through the pain he suddenly begins to feel the earth. After hundreds and hundreds of miles of walking, he begins to feel it. And he slowly starts to understands it.

Robert O'Hara points to a distant hillock and says aloud, 'I think I shall call this bluff Galways Bluff.'

'It may have a name already,' says King.

But Robert O'Hara doesn't hear him.

After two days' difficult journeying they are still by the banks of Coopers Creek. The nights are cold. But the men do not complain.

The last camel dies and they feed on its stringy flesh. Burke is angry. It is the camel he wanted to shoot. The one that had an illicit relationship with his beloved. Julia, wasn't it? He finds it hard to remember details.

The camel meat will sustain them for a small time. But now they have no means of carrying enough water. No means of reaching Mount Hopeless. They sit by the bank of the creek, their weary legs stretched out like dried-out sticks on the sand. And they wait for Mr Burke's guidance. But he won't even meet their eyes.

'What shall we do?' asks John Wills one morning.
   'We shall write our history,' the leader says firmly.
   'To what purpose?' asks Wills.
   'The historians always get it wrong.'
   'But we have no pen nor paper,' said Wills.
   'Use your journal,' says Robert O'Hara.
   'It's full.'
   'Then one of your other books. I know you have several.'
   'I think we ate them several hundred miles back.'
   Robert O'Hara frowns a moment and looks out at the horizon, as if seeking inspiration. 'Then I shall dictate it and you shall remember it,' he says.
   Wills nods. 'I shall do my best.'
   'Where shall I start?' asks Robert O'Hara. 'Perhaps at the point we left Melbourne, paraded by 30 cannon and three regiments of marching soldiers.'
   'Splendid,' says Wills. 'I have memorised it exactly.'

'Our triumph,' says Robert O'Hara talking slowly and carefully, 'was in finally reaching the gulf. We stepped out upon the white sands of the northern beaches, being the first white men to cross the continent. We mapped it and took possession of it in the name of Her Majesty and the Empire.'

He has to stop telling their history then. The emotion has quite overcome him.

'Where did we bury that food?' Robert O'Hara stirs and asks John Wills.

'What food?'

'There was roast partridge, and cranberries, and mangoes and quail, and I seem to remember salmon and red wine also.'

Wills looks at King. 'Do you know where we buried it, King?' he demands.

King, eager to please as ever, blinks a little then looks up at the sky. It is completely clear. Not a cloud in sight. As if you could see forever. 'I don't recall, sir,' he says, 'But I do remember burying Mr Gray.'

Robert O'Hara is looking around, studying the fading landscape fixedly. There's something wrong. Something missing.

'Where's young Mr King gone?' he suddenly asks.

'He went to look for the blacks,' says John Wills.

'Wretch! They'll probably spear him and feast on him.'

'He won't make much of a feast,' says Wills. 'Not enough of him.' Then he considers his own emaciated body. 'Still, he'd make better eating than us.'

Robert O'Hara doesn't like the thought of being eaten by blacks and looks across at Wills with an angry frown.

'Wills?' he calls. 'Where are you? Are you gone already?'

'I'm here,' says John Wills.

'I can't see you any more.'

'I'm just here.'

Robert O'Hara looks carefully. He can just make out his comrade's outline against the harsh light. 'You're fading away,' he says.

'And you're getting fainter,' says Wills. 'Harder to hear.'

'Then we'd best proceed with the story. Did we do the bit about reaching the ocean yet?'

'I don't think so.'

'Ah, well, we stood on the white sands of the gulf, surrounded by 50 cannons and five regiments of marching soldiers.'

'The blacks have given us food,' King says, arriving back at the camp.

'What blacks?' asks Robert O'Hara, feeling around for his pistol. But he can't see it. Can't even see Mr King.

'It's nardoo seed, sir,' King says. 'The blacks have taught me how to prepare it. They're very friendly.'

'Are they indeed?' asks Robert O'Hara. 'Well I don't want them being friendly around our camp. Tell them I have my gun here.'

'I think they don't want us to die,' says King.

'It's somewhere around here,' says Robert O'Hara, still searching.

'Do you think we'll ever get back to Melbourne?' asks John Wills.

'Of course!' says Robert O'Hara strongly. 'It's just beyond those mountains. If you listen you can hear the military band playing. They're waiting for us.'

Wills turns his ear to the wind. He hears the low murmur of the land. The sound of sand blowing over rocks. The sound of feet walking the land. He can hear for hundreds of miles. The sounds of millions of years.

'Yes,' he says, 'I think I can hear it.'

King prepared the nardoo paste for them with the slow determined pace of a sure survivor, and all three men ate it. It was filling enough, but it passed through them slowly and left them squatting in the sands, groaning as they endeavoured to pass monumental solid shits. They took hours to pass out of them and left them panting and exhausted.

After one particularly large stool John Wills climbed to his feet and said, 'I shall name that one Mount Hopeless.'

'It's the Queen's Birthday today,' says John Wills. Precise as ever.

'Hooray,' says Robert O'Hara. 'Gentlemen, I suggest we climb to our feet and propose a toast to her majesty.'

John Wills looks down at his legs. They will no longer support him. 'I don't think I can make it,' he says.

Robert O'Hara tries to struggle to his feet. But his legs prove treasonous too. 'Damnation!' he says. 'Damn-nation.'

He is silent for a while and then says, 'Never mind. Perhaps after supper.'

John Wills opens his eyes. Suddenly. He thought he was dead for a moment. He got a hell of a shock to see that heaven looked just like Coopers Creek. But then he knew he was still alive. Just.

'I think we shall die today,' he says.

'It doesn't matter,' says Robert O'Hara. 'We will live forever. When they find our bones the whole nation will mourn. Shops will close. Men and women will turn out in their mourning suits and line the streets of the cities. And they will cry for us. A flood of water to fill this parched desert.'

Robert O'Hara is completely still. But he's not dead yet. He's trying to recall something. Some vital detail of his grand history that he's forgotten.

He looks around for John Wills, but can't see him.

'Wills!' he calls.

'Yes,' comes the feeble reply.

'Do you recall what it was that was written on the tree at Coopers Creek. I can't quite make it out any more. There were some letters on the tree there. Did you read them?'

'Yes,' he says. 'I remember them.'

'Did we carve them there?' asks Robert O'Hara.

Wills thinks hard. 'Perhaps we did,' he says.
'What did they say?'
'I think it was our history.'
'Good man,' says Robert O'Hara. 'They won't forget us now!'

The Event of the Century

England, 1868

What the historian wrote:

'One of the most fascinating chapters in the story of Australian cricket is that of the visit to England by a team of Aborigines in 1868.'
(AG 'Johnnie' Moyes, *Australian Cricket — a History*, 1959)

What the journalist wrote:

'No arrival has been anticipated with so much curiosity and interest as that of the Black Cricketers from Australia ... they landed at Gravesend last Wednesday, and on the following day exhibited their cricket prowess at Town Malling, in Kent ... They are thirteen in number, and are captained by Charles Lawrence, late of the All-England Eleven, who has been for some time at the antipodes. We append their native names, and opposite is given their *soubriquets*, under which they will doubtless be known here.

Jungunjinanuke	Dick-a-Dick
Arrahmunijarrimun	Peter
Unaarrimin	Mullagh
Zellanach	Cuzens
Ballrinjarrimin	Sundown
Brippokei	King Cole
Bonmbarngeet	Tiger
Brimbunyah	Red Cap
Bullchanach	Bullocky
Grougarrong	Mosquito

Jallachmurrimin   Jim Crow
Murrumgunarriman   Twopenny
Pripumuarraman   Charley Dumas'
(*Sporting Life*, London, 16 May 1868)

What the historian wrote:

'One cannot but be fascinated by the thoughts of these men, many of whom lived in humpies on local properties near Lake Wallace, taking the field at Lord's, the first Australians to do so. I often wonder how they felt when playing against a team which included the Earl of Coventry, Viscount Downe, and Lieutenant Colonel Bathurst, who incidentally fell twice without scoring, each time to Cuzens.'
(Moyes, *Australian Cricket — a History*)

What the journalist predicted:

'Aboriginal play is a travesty upon cricket.'
(London *Times*, 1868)

What the spectator said:

They acquitted themselves very well and demonstrated a conspicuous skill at the game.
(WG Grace, 1899)

What the journalist wrote:

'The opening match was decidedly the event of the century.'
(*Sheffield Telegraph*, 1868)

What the historian wrote:

'During the tour Mullagh took five or more wickets in an innings 24 times. Lawrence, who took 261 wickets and made 1177 runs, had five or more 31 times, and twice had eight in an innings. Cuzens with 114 wickets and 1356 runs was clearly a fine player. Four times he got into the sixties, and he bowled very consistently. Another who had great days was Red Cap. Of course, the outstanding individual performance was that of Twopenny against East Hampshire. In 10 overs and two balls, he

took nine wickets for nine runs, eight of them bowled, and he caught the tenth batsman.'
(Moyes, *Australian Cricket — a History*)

What the anthropologist wrote:

'Active and lithe, they were never slow in play. They bowled with accuracy, involuntarily studying the wind as they raised their arm, as their fathers had studied it when about to hurl their spears ...'
(Daisy M Bates, *Australasian*, 1924)

What the historian wrote:

'Playing conditions which were more rigorous than those faced by modern touring sides also imposed difficulties and added strain. While matches normally lasted only two days, there were more of them, which added to the time spent travelling, often in uncomfortable transport. The hours of play were longer also than at present. Play began at 11 am or noon and usually continued until 7 pm or later.'
(DJ Mulvaney, *Cricket Walkabout*, 1967)

What the journalist wrote:

Contrary to general expectation, the Aboriginal team turned out to be a fine body of men, not only far removed from the low negro type of the *genus homo*, but able to 'take their own part' with well developed Europeans.
(*Sheffield Telegraph*, 1868)

What the historian wrote of what the journalists wrote:

'Sports writers attempted to describe the physical appearance of the Aborigines with an objectivity superior to that of many contemporary anthropologists.'
(Mulvaney, *Cricket Walkabout*)

What the journalist wrote:
'The men all had a smart, lively and gentlemanly appearance, which differed as much as the same number of Englishmen taken at random might vary.'
(*Newcastle Daily Chronicle*, 1868)

What the historian wrote:
'All the Aboriginal members of the team were given colours for identification purposes. Bullocky wore maroon, Cuzens white, Red Cap black, Mullagh dark blue, Tiger pink, Dick-a-Dick yellow, Twopenny drab, King Cole magenta, Peter green, and Dumas brown. King Cole died on tour and Mosquito took over his colours. Jim Crow used light blue.'
(Moyes, *Australian Cricket — a History*)

What the journalist wrote:
'They are the first Australian natives who have visited this country on such a novel expedition, but it must not be inferred that they are savages; on the contrary, the managers of the speculation make no pretence to anything other than purity of race and origin. They are perfectly civilised, having been brought up in the bush to agricultural pursuits as assistants to Europeans, and the only language of which they have a perfect knowledge is English. Monday in the Derby week is to witness their *debut* in London.'
(*Sporting Life*, London, 16 May 1868)

What the historian wrote:
'Mullagh seems to have been the star, as he scored more than 1685 runs, took 241 wickets and shone also as a wicket-keeper. His highest score was 94 in a match at Reading.'
(Moyes, *Australian Cricket — a History*)

What the anthropologist wrote:
'The aborigines were keener of sight, and made better and quicker play with their feet than their white fellow-cricketers.

Their fielding was marvellous, and their batting almost faultless ...'
(Bates, *Australasian*)

What the historian wrote:
'During the intervals in the games, the Aborigines often gave demonstrations of boomerang throwing and these sports interludes were very popular.'
(Moyes, *Australian Cricket — a History*)

What the spectator saw:
'Dick-a-Dick, the very popular member of the Australian cricketers who came to England in 1868, among other exhibitions of his quickness of eye and hand, allowed himself to be pelted with cricket-balls, at a distance of fifteen yards, having nothing wherewith to protect himself but the shield and the leowal, or angular club, the former being used to shield the body, and the latter to guard the legs. The force and accuracy with which a practised cricketer can throw the ball are familiar to all Englishmen, and it was really wonderful to see a man, with no clothes but a skin-tight elastic dress, with a piece of wood five inches wide in his left hand, and a club in his right, quietly stand against a positive rain of cricket-balls as long as any one liked to throw at him, and come out of the ordeal unscathed.'
(JG Wood, *The Natural History of Man*, 1870)

What the players saw:
'One match at the Oval in London attracted 7000 spectators, and over 5000 attended when they played at Sheffield in Yorkshire and Hove in Sussex.'
(*Illustrated History of Australia*, 1974)

What the journalist concluded:
'Nothing of interest comes from Australia except gold nuggets and black cricketers.'
(London *Daily Telegraph*, 13 May 1868)

What the historian wrote:
'On 4 February 1869, the *Dunbar Castle* docked at Sydney. With the exception of unfortunate King Cole, the team was back on Australian soil exactly a year after its departure.'
(Mulvaney, *Cricket Walkabout*)

What the journalist wrote:
'The aboriginal eleven has only lately returned to Sydney from the old country, where, under the captaincy of Mr Charles Laurence, they have played so many matches ... It is well known that the speculation has not been a very profitable one — in fact, has barely paid expenses, and we hope as considerable curiosity is felt to ascertain what progress the natives have made during their tour in England, there may be a good attendance of spectators to witness the play, and that the proceeds of the match, which will be given to the blacks, will be considerable.'
(*Australasian*, 20 February 1869)

What popular history recorded:
'An Australian party captained by WL Murdoch toured England in 1880. No matches were arranged against an England XI, the English still being unconvinced about the Aussies' ability at cricket, but CW Alcock, who was secretary of Surrey CCC, saw the possibilities of a game ... Now he arranged for England to play Australia at the Oval on 6, 7 and 8 September 1880, days which had originally been reserved for a match with Sussex. This match has taken its place in history as the first Test in England. England won by five wickets.'
(*The Ashes: A Complete Illustrated History*, 1990)

What history recorded that the journalist wrote:
'In affectionate Remembrance of English Cricket, which died at the Oval on 29th August 1882. Deeply lamented by a large circle of Friends and Acquaintances RIP. NB — the body will be cremated and the Ashes taken to Australia.'
(*Sporting Times*, 1882 — after the success of Australia's white touring team)

What the player wrote:
'I write to you with the intention of bringing under your notice that I have been working on the station this last six years. And never received any payment for the same doing Carpenter work. And I wish to let you know if they intend giving me any thing for my work I would prefer a double barreled gun for the money. I have made a bullock dray wheel for the dray. Please write as soon as convenient.
James Cousins.'
(Mosquito, Framlingham Aboriginal settlement, 2 June 1876)

What a solitary tombstone read:
'Johnny Mullagh — world famous cricketer. Born 1841. Died 14 August 1891.'
(Gravestone, Harrow cemetery)

What the historian wrote about what was not written:
'Unfortunately the cricketers were illiterate and their European backers failed to leave worthwhile records. While some of the team members had real character, their individuality is elusive.'
(Mulvaney, *Cricket Walkabout*)

What the lonely memorial reads:
'In this vicinity the Aboriginal Cricket Team, First Australian Cricket Team to tour England, trained prior to its departure in 1868.
  Matches Won 14
  Matches Lost 14
  Matches Drawn 19'
(Memorial at Lake Wallace, Edenhope, Victoria, unveiled 13 October 1951)

Ned Kelly Dreaming

Victoria, 1880

The black tracker looks at the ground, studies it a moment, then says, Four horses, gone that way. And he points up into the hills. Not with his hands, but with a turn of the head.

Captain Standish looks up towards the dark, thick bushland and sniffs uncomfortably.

'Are you sure?' he asks. He has no desire to go up into the ranges. To walk into one of the Kelly gang's bloody ambushes. To be shot in the remote bush, and fed on by the ants, like troopers Lonigan or Kennedy.

Four horses, says the black tracker again. That way. And he looks towards the ranges, deep into the dark trees.

Captain Standish turns up his collar, as if the chill of the winter's afternoon has descended upon him already. He makes no move to spur his horse onwards. Sits there looking at the ranges.

Silent.

'Shall we proceed then?' asks Lieutenant O'Connor, the Queenslander, eager for some sort of action.

But Standish doesn't answer him.

Ned examines his gun once more. Takes it slowly apart and peers at the campfire through each of the revolver's empty chambers. The others don't talk. Ned is moody this evening. Not to be messed with. A bad feeling has come upon him. Ned sees a fierce blaze shining at him through each chamber.

Suddenly there is a noise behind him in the darkness. He spins and points his revolver. His finger tightens on the trigger. Then realises it doesn't even have the chamber in it.

The other three men regard him. Slowly and carefully he places a cartridge in each chamber and reassembles the pistol. Then he holds it before him a moment longer. Then tucks it into his belt.

No. It wasn't them. When they came it would be without noise.

Captain Standish stirs the fire a little. Tries to see if the water is boiling. Says to O'Connor, 'I've been thinking. Perhaps we should send the blacks back to Queensland. Let it be known they have gone. That would bring the gang out of hiding.'

O'Connor says nothing. He knows his troopers could find the Kelly gang if only Standish would allow them. He also knows that Standish is deathly afraid of going into the ranges. He can see it in his eyes. The hate and the fear that drives him.

O'Connor nods a little. Says nothing. Sees the water is beginning to boil. Then says, 'Do you know what they say in Benalla? They say that the black troopers are unhappy because I will not let them eat the bushrangers when we catch them.'

Standish's face looks quite white in the light of the small campfire.

'Are they truly cannibals?' he asks. Very slowly. 'I have heard such.'

Again O'Connor chooses not to answer.

Ned is unable to sleep. He walks away from the campfire into the chill embrace of the night. Those six little devils are out there somewhere. Tracking him. They can see where he has walked on rock. They can see where a man has touched a sapling, by the specks of salt crystals left by a sweaty hand. They can identify tracks on the floor of a creek bed. They are men who know the land. Are not afraid of it.

NED KELLY DREAMING

Ned has spent some time with the local Yarralin people before. He knows how they live off the land. Knows how they live with the land. Knows how they move through it like shadows.

The very rocks and leaves around him are telling them his path. The land is betraying him to them. He fears no policeman alive. But he fears the black trackers.

Captain Standish can't sleep. It is fearfully cold. Chill fingers dig into his kidneys. He is wrapped in three blankets. Huddled close to the fire. He nods off. Dreams fitfully, then wakes again.

The blacks sit around their own fire. Chanting.

'Dammit!' says Standish. 'Can't you make them stop? They're keeping me awake.' He shakes O'Connor until he stirs and then says it again.

'It's the land,' says O'Connor. 'They don't know it.'

'What do you mean don't know it? They're blacks!'

'Their land is near Mackay and Fraser Island. They don't know this land. Don't know the stories about it. Don't know how to walk it, they say.'

'That's absurd,' says Standish.

'And the cold,' says O'Connor. 'Since Corporal Sambo died of consumptive cough, they fear that the cold and the night bring death somehow.'

'You mean they fear the dark!' barks Standish and laughs.

'Don't we all?' asks O'Connor, and rolls back into his blanket.

Ned is fast asleep at last. He dreams he is striding across the land. Walking from one end of Kelly country to the other. Walking its boundaries, taking huge steps. Like a giant. Then he comes to the camp of the Yarralin people, as he did so many years ago. But now they are wretched and living in squalor, poorer even than his own people.

He sits amongst them and boils a billy of tea. He bakes damper in the ashes of the fire. And despite the large numbers of people in the tribe, the many people of his own family, and their neighbours from the hills around Benalla and Glenrowan, there is enough tea and damper to feed them all.

Then the tribe is gone. His people gone. And he is surrounded by police. Guns drawn. Firing. Each chamber filled with fire. And then he is burning. The fire consuming him. Sending him up into the sky in flying sparks. Like stars in the night.

Stanhope O'Connor is far from the cold ranges tonight. He is in the small back room of Craven's Hotel in Benalla, with Louisa Smith, the beautiful young woman to whom Standish had introduced him. And then later confided to him that she was his intended.

The chill of the Victorian winter's night barely touches him as he holds her in his arms. There are no lights in the back room, but the soft whiteness of her breasts seems to him like the bright moonlight of his home in the north. It illuminates her whole body.

He has followed her around the hotel for half the afternoon as she left subtle signs and tracks for him to follow, her face impassive, but her eyes full of inviting danger.

She is warm to the touch. She whispers urgently into his ear and kisses him with a fiery passion. Lets him slowly run his hands under her skirts. Exploring in the darkness.

Back in his own bedroom he finds blood on his hands. And he no longer wishes to slay the bushrangers. To track them will prove him enough. And then when he returns to Queensland he will take her with him, he thinks.

On some nights, out in the bush, the thought of her seems more like a dream than a memory. And each time he looks at Standish he wonders to himself, does he know?

Captain Standish is tired and irritable. It is a chill morning, before dawn. Stars are still in the sky.

He saddles his horse slowly. Waiting for O'Connor to brew a cup of tea. The lieutenant comes over to him and says, 'The men say he was here last night.'

'What?' asks Standish, blinking in disbelief. 'What?'

'The troopers say he was here last night.'

'Who?' demands Standish, though he already knows. But needs for O'Connor to say it. To name him.

'Kelly,' says O'Connor.

Standish leaves the horse and strides over to the black trackers. Still huddled around their fire.

'You there,' he says to the nearest one, pointing at him. 'You there, Sambo.'

'No sir,' says O'Connor. 'He was the one who died. They don't say his name. That trooper there is called Hero.'

'Hero, hmmm?' asks Standish. He addresses the man again. 'What do you mean he was here?' The black looks up and puckers his lips. Like a kiss. But he does it to indicate direction.

'Where?' asks Standish. 'Where are the tracks. Show me! Show me!' he shouts. Again the black puckers his lips to one side.

'Point!' snaps Standish. 'Point to them!' The black stands, wipes his hands on his rough blue uniform and walks slowly across to a rocky outcrop.

These his tracks, says the trooper called Hero, indicating the rocks. Standish follows him closely. Examines the ground carefully.

Just 'ere, says trooper Hero. He waves at an indentation in the rock. And over there, says another black. He doesn't point either. He stands in front of a rock formation on the ground and indicates its shape.

Standish looks at the men carefully. Tries to understand what they are telling him.

'Ned Kelly was here?' he asks again. 'The man we're after?'

Yes, says one trooper.

No, says another. Nedkelly rode 'ere. But not that fella we chasin'. This another one. This one ten foot tall. Maybe twenty.

Then a third black says, he come past walking. Taking big steps. Big. And he himself takes a big step to demonstrate.

These his tracks, says trooper Hero, indicating the rocks again.

Standish puts his hand on the rock. 'What do you mean?' he asks. But he starts to understand. These men are more afraid of the outlaw than he is, he thinks.

Standish turns to look at them. 'He walked there last night, did he?' he asks, as if he's talking to little children.

Yes, says Hero. Last night. Long time ago. Been 'ere long, long time before.

Standish nods slowly. Sighs. 'And are they the only tracks you have found?'

More, says trooper Hero. He been this way. Close now. He be staying 'ere some time.

'How long?' asks O'Connor.

Long time. Forever.

'Show me other tracks,' demands Standish. 'Real tracks.'

Up there, says Hero and points at the fading stars. You see 'im. Show his trail. Been there forever.

Standish strides back to his horse. Leaves the blacks looking at the rocks. He has already decided not to pay them their promised £3 each. They'd be better back in Queensland.

Captain Standish leads the party through the bush, following the track back to Wangaratta. He is stiff and sore. He is thinking of the warm beds in the hotel room, and a warm meal.

Lieutenant O'Connor rides behind him. And the five black trackers ride in a single line behind him. O'Connor is thinking of going back to Queensland with the black mounted troopers.

He wants to see the bushrangers caught, but he is sick of being kept on Standish's tight leash. The man is ill-suited to this task, he thinks. He looks up and sees his superior stop and turn back to him, a cold look on his face, as if he knows what he is thinking.

Captain Standish lets O'Connor catch up to him and then he gently spurs his horse on, riding beside him.

'I've been thinking,' says Standish. 'We'll never catch the Kellys by marching around in the ranges. What we need is a trap. Some way we can lure the outlaws into town. Make them fight on our terms. Against a strong contingent of heavily armed police.'

He glances at O'Connor for comment, but receives none.

'We need to bring him into the open,' says Standish. 'Surround him and shoot him down like a dog. That will mark the end of him and his kind.'

O'Connor doesn't answer. He wishes for a large fire to warm the morning's chill. Wishes he were with Louisa again. Wishes he were heading back home to Queensland with his men. But he will stay on until the bushrangers are caught. He will see the chase out.

He wants to corner Ned Kelly and look into his eyes. Wants to see what his fears and dreams are.

Then Standish asks, 'What did the blacks mean about seeing his tracks in the stars?'

And O'Connor looks up to the sky. Wonders if the bushranger is looking up at the heavens at that moment too. Looking for an answer there. But there are no more stars to be seen.

Mrs Watson Escapes the Cannibals

Lizard Island, northern Queensland, 1881

Mrs Watson looks up over the edge of the large iron cooking pot. There is water as far as she can see.

'I think we're safe now,' she says. But her Chinese servant, Ah Sam, does not reply. He is lying in the bottom of the pot, trying not to bleed onto any of Mrs Watson's valuable possessions.

She wonders if he heard her. Perhaps she should repeat herself. Wonders if it might bring him some cheer. But he closes his eyes and turns his head away a little.

That is the trouble with the Chinese, she thinks. They are so inscrutable.

So she lifts her young baby, Ferrier, up high and shows him the sea. 'Look,' she says, 'No cannibals in sight. We are quite safe now.'

The baby coos brightly. But Ah Sam only groans and slumps a little lower in the pot.

No stamina, she thinks. Four spear wounds and he thinks he is dying! A white man would never complain like that. She's suffering from thirst very badly herself. But she doesn't loll about the cooking pot complaining and groaning.

Yet she does wish she were back in Ipswich, where the heat was bearable. Where you couldn't even see the ocean. And where there was some manner of white civilisation. But Mrs Mary Watson knows she is a long, long way from Ipswich, and they have a long way still to go in their floating cooking pot before they are truly safe.

'We're not out of the hot water yet,' she says.

She turns her head and looks back the way they have come. Sees Lizard Island faintly in the distance. Dark against the late afternoon light. She is glad to be free of it. She had told her husband she was happy there. But it had always unsettled her. The heat. The toil. And the lizards. Always the lizards. Tiny skinks. Large lizards. Lizards everywhere. Under rocks. On the steps. On the walls of their home. Lying about like so many dark and troubling thoughts, discarded and brought to life. Dark slithering creatures that turned her skin to gooseflesh and crawled silently into her dreams.

The lizards were bad. But they weren't as bad as the blacks. They had always been the real menace. Lurking in the bushes. Watching but never seen. Arriving by night in their canoes. Peering at her from the darkness. Making wild animal sounds and then slithering away when her husband went hunting for them.

She had written in her diary before they fled the island: '*Ah Sam saw smoke in S direction, supposed to be from natives camp.*'

That's when she knew they'd returned. Her husband, the goodly Mr Bob Watson, told her that the island had once been sacred to them. Said it had been told to him, as he had been told they were cannibals. Said they had ancient rock formations. She had seen them. Circles of rocks, quite near their homestead. She'd stood there and walked carefully around them, wondering what strange meaning they possessed. She had walked through the centre of the ring of rocks and wondered why a shiver ran down her neck, turned her skin to gooseflesh.

'Someone has walked over my grave, they would have said in Cornwall,' she says aloud. As if to Ferrier. As if to Ah Sam. As if to herself. It is so hot. And she is so thirsty. Just a sip of water would ease the thirst. Just one more sip.

Ah Sam opens his eyes and looks to her. Watches her. He raises himself a little and peers over the edge of the cooking pot. He sees the ocean. Sees it stretching away before them. Then slumps back down again.

She can see his lips are dried and cracked too. Knows he also needs a mouthful of water. But their water has given out. She had packed so carefully before their escape. Tinned meat. Her jewellery. Preserved milk. The revolver. The account books. But water! Of all the things to forget.

And she remembers her husband, the hard-working Mr Bob Watson, once telling her that lizards did not need to drink. That they could take in moisture through their scaled skins. If she were a lizard she would be all right, she thinks.

She turns her head away from Lizard Island and looks towards the Howick Islands. She hopes their drift will continue to take them in that direction. They will find water there, surely. She wonders how long it might take them to reach the islands. Wonders how soon it will be until dark. Wonders if the new day might bring rain clouds towards them. Wishes for rain. Wonders if drinking sea water is really as dangerous as her husband has said. Surely not just a sip. Just to moisten the lips. Surely.

The fierce heat of day will begin to fade soon, she thinks. The iron pot against her back will turn cold then. Sending a chill down her spine.

She is glad the cannibals have not come after them in their canoes. She thinks how pleased they would have been to have caught them in a cooking pot. They would have towed them back to Lizard Island and hoisted them over a fire.

She wonders if the cannibals knew that the iron tank she was floating in was a cooking pot. Surely. They must have spied her husband and Ah Sam and Ah Leong boiling up bêche-de-mer in it at some time. It was the bêche-de-mer that took them to Lizard Island. Her husband, the entrepreneurial Mr Bob Watson, said it would assure their fortunes. They would return to Cairns with riches and prosperity. She would be freed from having to labour as a teacher of ignorant and spoilt children. She liked his promises. Liked the words he whispered in her ears at night as she lay beside him in bed. Wealth and security. A few hard years, he'd said, and then they would return to civilisation. Set up for life. His hands and his promises slithered slowly under her night garments. Turned her skin to gooseflesh.

But the bêche-de-mer had given out too quickly. After their son Ferrier was born, her husband, the hapless Mr Bob Watson, had gone north for two months, looking for new bêche-de-mer grounds. Leaving her and the two Chinese coolies to cope. That was the measure of a capable woman in the colonies, she thought. How well she coped.

But when her husband was gone the cannibals returned. Lurking in the darkness. Watching but never seen. Calling out wild animal sounds. Dancing around their rock circles. Dreaming of the taste of white flesh.

She had written in her diary: '*Natives down on the beach at 7 pm. Fired off rifle and revolver and they went away.*'

Ferrier starts whimpering and she puts a hand on his forehead. He is warm. Perhaps he is getting a fever. She wishes she had something to give him. Keeping a careful eye on Ah Sam, she exposes one pale breast and offers it to her son. He takes it greedily. She leans back against the iron of the pot and lets him feed. It is, as ever, a comforting feeling. Quite pleasurable.

She has heard that Chinamen could go wild at the sight of a white woman's breast. Heavens knows her husband certainly did. Then she wonders how the cannibals would have reacted. She has heard that once a black cannibal had tasted white flesh they would settle for nothing else. Like they said that once a white man had slept with a black woman he would settle for nothing else. She wonders what the black women did that made them so appealing. Perhaps they were more willing to perform base acts. Take the man in their mouths. She thinks that it must surely be terribly foolhardy of any man to engage in such practices with a cannibal woman, no matter what the pleasure.

Then she wonders which part of a person the cannibals most preferred. She wonders which bits of her they might feast on. Her thighs? Her breasts? Plenty of meat on both. The thought sends a shiver down her neck.

'Somebody walked on my grave again,' she says to Ferrier, still feeding at her breast.

Ah Sam stirs a little at her voice. She looks at his long thin limbs. Wonders what kind of a meal he would make. Surely too stringy and tough. And she wonders how the cannibals ate poor Ah Leong. Did they roast him on a fire or chop him up and eat him raw? She looks across at Ah Sam and imagines his companion's legs and arms dismembered and smouldering in a fire.

And she wonders which bits of a Chinaman might be more highly prized. The hands? Too bony. The buttocks? Surely not. The ears? The privates? In Cornwall, in her youth, she remembers that rams' testicles were often cooked as a treat.

And she remembers writing in her diary: '*Ah Leong killed by the blacks over at the farm. Ah Sam found his hat which is the only proof.*'

Ferrier is now asleep again. Ah Sam groans a little and his foot twitches. Mary Watson watches him, then looks around for her diary. She will write up these thoughts. She searches amongst the small pile of things she has brought. Looks for the small book. But it is not there. She could have sworn it was there earlier. Perhaps she had left it behind on Lizard Island. Perhaps the cannibals are sitting over it, at this very instant, pondering the words she has written. Trying to make sense of the strange shapes and ciphers. Trying to make sense of the story of the death of poor Ah Leong. Trying to understand why she had fired over their heads when she could easily have shot them. And in truth she had thought of it. But there were too many. And she knew a shot in the air would suffice. As it did for the lizards. One shot and they slithered for cover. The slimy beasts.

A lizard does not need water, she thinks again. Imagines she is a lizard herself. And she has a thought that perhaps the beasts on Lizard Island were created from the thousands of souls, like herself and Ah Sam, who have been stranded without fresh water and prayed and wished for some deliverance. And by some strange whim of the gods they had become lizards. And she wonders what kind of lizard she would be. A large monitor, or a small skink? She is not sure she likes the idea. To be brought so low that she should ever wish to be a lizard!

She reaches over the side of the cooking pot and takes a small sip of sea water. Just one more. Just to wet her lips. Just to moisten them. She can't understand how it could be so dangerous. She would like to have been able to ask her husband, the all-knowing Mr Bob Watson, to please explain.

Mary Watson has a strong need to write down these thoughts, and wishes again that she had her diary with her. Of all the things to forget. But certainly it was her diary that had saved them, she thinks. Because the blacks were distracted by it and had not taken up the opportunity to pursue them. They sat in her house that very instant, turning over the pages, trying to decipher the spells and magic written there, while she escaped. Surely that was it.

She opens up one of the account books she has brought and rips out a sheet of paper. She will create a new diary. She will record how capably she has coped. Perhaps she will be able to write a book about it that will ensure her and her husband's prosperity. It will sell very well both in the colonies and at home. She will tell of the dangerous life of a settler's wife. Of the inscrutability of the Chinese. Of the treachery and cannibalism of the blacks. It will be a book from which all white people will take heart and courage.

She writes: '*Left Lizard Island September 2nd 1881 (Sunday afternoon). Got about three miles or four from the Lizards.*'

She stops. Tries to remember if it is September or October. It had been very clear to her just a moment ago. She is parched. Needs a sip of water to go on. Just one more.

'*September 4 — Made for the sand bank off the Lizards, but could not reach it. Got on a reef.*'

That covered the last two days. Now she should address the present. She concentrates a moment. Trying to grasp everything that has happened to her today. Everything she has thought. Tries to put it into words. But it is too hard to recapture her thoughts. It is as if they slither away and float off on the waves. Just out of her reach.

She writes: '*September 5 — Remained on the reef all day on the lookout for a boat but saw none.*'

She puts the pencil and paper down. Ferrier is waking up. Crying a little. He is still hot. Perhaps if she bathes him in sea water. She reaches up and gathers a small amount in her hand

and applies it gently to his cheeks. There is so much of Bob in his face, she thinks. But you had to look carefully to see it, as if it was hiding there. The water soothes Ferrier a little. She rocks him until he returns to sleep. Ah Sam is snoring now. Also asleep. He should at least be fishing or steering, she thinks. Or he could take one of the paddles and row. Her husband will be angry at him when he finds out how lazy he has been. Four spear wounds and he thinks he's dying!

Then she closes her own eyes and rests. She is suddenly very tired. Perhaps it is the heat. Or the lack of water. Maybe just one more sip.

Suddenly the pot strikes something hard. Ah Sam groans. Mary Watson peers carefully over the side. 'Bother,' she says. They are on a reef of some kind. The reef of which she has just written. Perhaps they will float free again. She tries to remember if the tide is coming in or out. Tries to remember if she had written about this in her diary on Lizard Island. There was something about striking rocks. Tries to remember the shape of the rocks in the sacred ring. Tries to remember the exact features of her husband's face.

Tries to remember if she has already written what will happen the next day?

September 6 — Very calm morning. Able to pull the tank up to an island with three small mountains on it. Ah Sam went ashore to try and get water, as ours was done. There were natives camped there, so we were afraid to go far away. We had to wait return of tide. Anchored under the mangroves; got on a reef. Very calm.

Then she wonders what she will prepare for their meal on that day. She will feed Ferrier on preserved milk again. And perhaps Ah Sam can dig us some vegetables. She wonders if the blacks have trampled the vegetable garden? Planted Ah Leong's bones there to grow anew. Wonders what he will grow like. What shaped plant would a Chinaman grow into? What would he taste like? Or perhaps Ah Sam could catch a fish, she thinks. And she remembers a story she once heard in Cornwall about a hungry fisherman, sitting in his boat wishing for prosperity and for food. And a fish suddenly jumped into his boat. And there was a gold coin in its mouth. That's what will happen to her. They will have food and money. And her book will be a bestseller. It will make their fortune. Like the bêche-de-mer never could. And it will rain in the morning. Large black clouds will fill the sky and fill the pot with fresh water. But they will have found land first. Just when they are at the very end of their tether. That would be more dramatic, she thinks.

> *September 7 — Made for another island four or five miles from the one spoken of yesterday. Ashore, but could not find any water. Cooked some rice and clam-fish. Moderate SE breeze. Stayed here all night. Saw a steamer bound north. Hoisted Ferrier's white and pink wrap but did not answer us.*

Yes. That's good she thinks. The steamer sailing so close to them. Waving her poor child's coat high in the air. The cruelty of being so close to salvation and not being sighted. What mother could read those lines and not feel a beat of sadness in her breast. That's what would happen. But first they will have to get off the reef, she thinks. Free from the rocks. The circle of rocks. A circle of lizards. Peering at her. Immobile. They would absorb water through their skin. Enough to float free on.

> *September 8 — Changed the anchorage of the boat as the wind was freshening. Went down to a kind of little lake on the same island (this done last night). Remained here all day looking out for a boat; did not see any. Very cold night; blowing very hard. No water.*

Just the sea water. But only ever a sip. Just to wet the lips. Just to moisten the skin. Just one more.

> *September 9 — Brought the tank ashore as far as possible with this morning's tide. Made camp all day under the trees. Blowing very hard. No water. Gave Ferrier a dip in the sea; he is showing symptoms of thirst, and I took a dip*

myself. Ah Sam and self very parched with thirst. Ferrier showing symptoms.

She wonders if Ah Sam will die in her story. And she wonders if she will have to eat him. Wonders what he will taste like. Wonders which bits of him she will take into her mouth first. Wonders if she can cook him. Or eat him raw. Then plant the bones to grow a garden of little Chinaman's limbs for her and her child to live on.

September 10 — Ferrier very bad with inflamation; very much alarmed. No fresh water, and no more milk, but condensed. Self very weak; really thought I would have died last night (Sunday).

She thinks of her book. Of what will happen next. She will dream of death. Will dream of rescue. Her husband sailing back from the north. Jumping into the pot with a gold coin in his mouth. Riches and prosperity. They will sail away together in the pot. To Ipswich. Or to the home country. That will be the ending of the book.

But what will be her final words? Something that will take her right to the edge of death before she is found. Something that will show how slim a line there is between life and death. How few pencil strokes separate illusions and reality.

September 11 — Still all alive. Ferrier much better this morning. Self feeling very weak. I think it will rain today, clouds very heavy, wind not quite so hard. No rain. Morning fine weather. Ah Sam preparing to die. Have not seen him since 9. Ferrier more cheerful. Self not feeling at all well. Have not seen any boat of any description. No water. Near dead with thirst.

And then it will rain, she thinks. It will rain and rain and rain. Filling the cooking pot. Filling it with fresh water. Right to the brim. Right over her head.

And that is how they will find her.

KRAO

The "Missing Link"

Living proof of Darwin's theory of the descent of man

THE WONDER OF WONDERS

The usual argument against the Darwinian theory, that man and monkey had no common origin, has always been that no animal has hitherto been discovered in the transmission state between monkey and man.

"KRAO"

A perfect specimen of the step between man and monkey, discovered in Laos

ALL SHOULD SEE HER

KRAO — The Missing Link

Barnum's Great Ethnological Congress of Curious People From All Parts of the World, 1892

There are savages all around me. Dressed in the furs of dead animals. Screeching wildly. Baring their teeth menacingly at me. But the cage protects me. They press up close to the bars. Roll their eyes at me. I retreat to the far corner of my cage and stare back at them.

Listen to them. Jibber, jibber, jibber. Savages! They make me sick. Always screeching and laughing.

They stand there and read the sign over my cage.

KRAO — THE "MISSING LINK"

That's me. Krao the monkey-woman. There is a large billboard out the front of my cage asking

WHAT IS IT?

And the savages press up against the bars and try to guess. Is she a monkey? Is she human? Then they read the fading poster in full.

The savages stand there and read the details over and over. Then look at me again. They laugh and jibber some more and move on to the next exhibit.

But they fall silent as they stand at that cage beside mine. The sign reads

AUSTRALIAN CANNIBALS

but there are no Australians there any more. They have gone. The savages stand before the empty cage, reading the sign, trying to figure out what it all means.

But all they see is that I am the missing link — and the Australians are simply missing.

A Tribe of Male and Female Australian Cannibals

Also known as bushmen, black trackers and Boomerang throwers, these are the only ones of their monstrous, self-disfigured and hopelessly embruited race, ever lured from the remote, unexplored and dreadful interior wilds, where they wage an endless war of extermination, that they may gratify their hellish appetite and gorge themselves upon each other's flesh.

I like seeing the disappointment on the savages' faces at missing the thrill of standing so close to wild cannibals. And they read the sign again and try to picture what they must have looked like. They try to create them in their own minds. But they'll never know.

Or they shrug and walk down the row to the cage where the Fijian Cannibals are. Then their faces light up. Real cannibals! With black skin and frizzy hair and sharp teeth! Although one of the women is really a negress from Alabama. They'll never know that either. She puts on a good show though. And the Circassian Beauty in the cage next to the Fijian Cannibals, who is claimed to have been rescued from a Turkish Harem, she was actually rescued from the New York slums.

She will sit primly in her cage until we reach Hannibal, Ohio. The end of the line for the circus. Then she will be unemployed once more. She will probably take up drinking again and die young. Or end up in another 'harem', a long way from home. And next year Mr Barnum will rescue another Circassian Beauty in New York.

It will not be so easy to obtain new Australians, however. Mr Cunningham, the man-hunter, travelled halfway around the world to that strange country at the bottom of the globe to find some specimens to lure back to Mr Barnum's circus. There were nine of them. Dark and fierce looking. But very gentle when you got to know them.

I miss them. Miss their songs. Miss their stories. They used to dance and sing their strange low chants at night, and clap their boomerang sticks together, and I would close my eyes and almost imagine their distant homeland. So far from these cold mid-western plains. Dry and warm underfoot. Embracing them in its heat.

As their songs drifted into my sleep I imagined they were seeking to recreate their homeland amongst the sawdust and manure of the circus. I never understood the words they sang, but at times, half asleep, I felt the chanting working its power on me, and I would smell the warm breeze off the ocean and smell the sand and tropical foliage of their distant homeland all about me.

Tambo, one of the young Australians, who spoke English well, told me that their land was created by a huge carpet snake that slithered down from the mountainous hinterland, creating the rivers and islands. How Mr Barnum would have loved to have had that snake in his circus. But he has me.

KRAO — THE "MISSING LINK"

There is a handbill stuck on the wall of my cage, that shows me climbing a jungle tree. I am depicted as a small hairy woman-ape, wearing nothing but a loin cloth and ornate wrist bands. My body is covered in short hair from head to foot. They used to give out the handbill in all the small towns we visited. It would draw the crowds. But they would look disappointed when they saw me. For while I am certainly hairy, I am not quite as close to a monkey in form as the handbill would have them believe. In fact, when I don my dress and veil and walk about the towns I am so normal as to be ignored. But here in my cage, in the world of Mr Barnum, I am neither woman nor monkey. I am Krao. I am — what is it? The missing link.

And the land of the Australians that they have painted onto their poster, it is not the land I dreamed of when they were singing. It shows palm trees and a jungle clearing and wild men hurling sticks and arrows at each other. That is a land of Mr Cunningham and Mr Barnum's invention.

The Australians came to the circus in Baltimore, soon after we had begun the 1883 season. Every few nights was a new town. A new show. A new hoard of savages peering in at us. Then we would move onto the train and on to the next town. The list of towns goes on and on, year after year. I knew them all by heart. Baltimore to Washington to Martinsbury, Cumberland, Wheeling, Zanesville, Newark, Columbus, Springfield, Dayton, Cincinatti, Hamilton, Richmond, Indianapolis, St Louis, Chicago, La Porte, South Bend, Coldwater, Adrian, Jackson, Battle Creek, Kalamazoo …

I learned the names of all the Australians. Tambo. His young wife Sussy. Toby and Jenny and their son Little Toby. And there were four other men: Bob, Wangon, Billy and Jimmy. They were not tall. But they stood proud when alone. They had wild heads of frizzy hair like the Fijians, but differed in that the chests of the men were scarred deeply in long horizontal scars. Initiation marks, Tambo told me. The savages were fascinated by them.

I learned that the Australians came from different tribes and had no language in common as a group, but some English. But Cunning Cunningham didn't like them mixing with others. He tried to keep them to himself. He was the one who put the bones through their noses. Posed with them for photographs. Made sure their fees were paid in his name.

Mr Cunningham went to Australia a year or so before he brought the Australians to the circus. He was unashamedly hunting for specimens for Mr Barnum's circus. And when he saw the native black people of that land he knew he had hit upon a minor fortune.

The Australians told me that he had first travelled to a northern city named after Mr Charles Darwin, to whom I begrudgingly owe my own livelihood, to capture some 'wild boomerang throwers'. But the authorities of that city prevented him from doing so. So he kept travelling, knowing from experience that the right men, with the right belief in his words or his money, would be found, sooner or later.

Tambo and his wife and the seven other Australians came from islands off the coast of the colony of Queensland. Cunning Cunningham persuaded them to join him.

They arrived cold and a little bewildered. I watched Cunningham tend to their needs. He fed them. Dressed them. Instructed them in how to alter their dances for the crowds. And then he watched them take their place with us in Mr Barnum's Great Ethnological Congress of Curious People From All Parts of the World.

We introduce In America the first band taken
AUSTRALIAN BOOMERANG THROWERS

Queensland black trackers and ranting man eaters — the celebrated bushmen from the continent on the other side! The only captive band of these ferocious, treacherous and uncivilised savages, with deep scars and seams in the tortured flesh, and bones and huge rings thrust through their noses and ears as ornaments. Veritable blood-thirsty beasts in distorted human form, with but a glimmering of reason and gift of speech. They will be introduced in their peace, war, kangaroo and emu dances, their midnight corro-beries, casting of the waddy and whirling of the boomerang, worth journeying 100 miles to see these specimens of the

LOWEST ORDER OF MAN

And they were good showmen, I'll give them that. They put on a first-class performance. Dancing and mock fighting. But they only sang at nights. Sang for their homeland perhaps. Or for their families. I don't know. I can only imagine.

The part of their act that always raised the crowd's interest was the boomerang throwing.

THE BOOMERANG

A crescent-shaped club of hardest wood, which is made to reverse the accepted laws of projection and gravitation. It is not thrown at, but from the object, it is destined to return and strike, with unerring skill and crushing force. No other people have ever been able to master this extraordinary weapon.

Tambo would take a boomerang and hurl it towards the crowd, and it would spin out across the centre of the circus ring, as if it was going to hack into those seated in its path — and they would throw up their arms and gasp in fright. But then it would begin enacting the most curious change in its flight, and would turn in the air, moving in an arc, and would return to Tambo. He would reach up and just pluck it out of the air. It was truly amazing to watch. And try as they might none of the other circus performers could ever make the boomerang return to them with the same skill.

In the parades the Australians wore rough animal skins and went half naked, carrying their boomerangs under their arms. But in private they liked to dress well. Tambo was fond of a top hat and cane. He was wearing one when we reached Cleveland, Ohio.

It was a cold winter and we toured by rail. Boxed up in little cars like cattle. Unloaded and paraded in each small city in the mid-west and right up into Canada. We passed through Montreal and Ottawa, Brockville, Kingston, Hamilton, Brantford, Woodstock, St Thomas, London, Chatham, Toledo, Defiance, Tiffin, Mansfield, Lancaster, Washington, Chillicothe, Portsmouth, Gallipolis, Parkesburg, Marietta, Pittsburgh, Youngstown, Steubenville, Canton, Akron and reached Cleveland in February 1884.

The Australians all had chest infections by then. Tambo's became pneumonia. And he was the first to die.

His wife Sussy was grief stricken. For months after, if you even mentioned his name she would start crying and sobbing. She missed him terribly. But she was fortunate to have had a husband. Many of us here will never know what it is like to live with our own kind. Or to die amongst them and to be mourned by them.

There are no other missing links to miss me when I die.

Cunningham got nervous of course. He imagined that all his capital would start dying. So he took them to Europe. Maybe he thought he could make more money there before they died on him.

I knew the other Australians wanted Tambo's body. But he told them it had been buried. That was another fantasy world he created. I later heard that he had it embalmed and placed in a dime museum in Cleveland, where visitors could examine the dark tones of the skin. See the large chest scars. Study the heavy brow and forehead and shake their heads at the primitive savage displayed before them.

They could have saved their dime and looked in a mirror.

I'd like to think that in another age Cunningham, the man-hunter, would be put in a cage, and the many hundred peoples whom he and his kind have kidnapped over the years would come and stare at him. He would be dressed in his heavy dark coat, with his long thick beard and maddened eyes, staring out fearfully at those who pressed up close to regard him. The thousands who had lost family and friends to him and his like. And they would shake their heads to imagine that such a savage image of humanity should exist.

AUSTRALIAN BUSHMEN
UNDERSIZED AND DISTORTED IN FORM

With bestiality, ferocity and treachery stamped upon their faces; their cruel eyes reflecting but a glimmering of reason; having no gift of speech beyond an ape-like gibberish, utterly unintelligible to anyone else; they are but one step removed from brutes in human form and

BEYOND CONCEPTION MOST CURIOUS TO LOOK UPON

I was told that seven of the Australians survived the journey to Europe and were put on display in the Crystal Palace in

London. That tall glass and metal cage that I have seen in photos. I imagine them standing there amongst the stuffed animals and tropical pot plants and mannequins. Statues and models of Sioux Indians and Nubians and Zulus. Great African beasts. Living in a world of glass, created by some man like Mr Barnum or Mr Cunningham. An absurd mix of trees and ferns, creating a tropical jungle that exists nowhere else other than in his mind. And they lived in that world. Like living mannequins. Growling for the crowds. Watching the thousands of visitors press up close, baring their teeth at them. Reading the placards and moving on.

And I wonder if the Australians ever pressed their faces up against the glass there? Felt its chill touch on their skin as they looked at the cold grey world outside? And did they still sing their songs at night?

Or did they think of Tambo? His body was now mummified and preserved like one of the mannequins around them. Far from his homeland. With no-one to create it for him in song and dance. No way of ever returning to it without his people.

Cunningham took them on to Europe, while Barnum's Great Ethnological Congress of Curious People From All Parts of the World continued its tour. We went on to Norwalk, Fremont, Lima, Piqua, Nuncie, Lexington, Louisville, Lafeyette, Logansport, Fort Wayne, Evansville, Vincennes, Terre Haute, Danville, Decatur, Jacksonville, Bloomington, Peoria, Ottawa, Joliet, Aurora, Rockford, Janesville, Madison, Watertown, Milwaukee, Ford du Lac, Oshkosh, Stevens Point, Eau Clarie, Stillwater, St Paul, Minneapolis, Dubuque, Waterloo, Cedar Rapids, Rock Island, Galesburg, Burlington, Des Moines, Ottumwa, Keokuk, Quincy, Louisiana and finally Hannibal, Ohio. The end of the line for the circus. The end of the season. The end of the Circassian Beauty. Another specimen lost forever. Another specimen to be created anew the next year.

I'm told the Australians were toured from Moscow to Constantinople. Mr Cunningham, the man-hunter, took them to strange lands and strange exhibition halls where they would never feel the touch of tropical sand nor the scent of the warm breeze off the ocean.

And one by one they died, until they too existed only as photographs or mannequins or figures sketched on handbills.

And I'm told that Cunning Cunningham has gone back to Australia to find more cannibal boomerang throwers to join us for next year's season. They will probably use the old handbills.

A Tribe of Male and Female Australian Cannibals

Also known as bushmen, black trackers and Boomerang throwers, these are the only ones of their monstrous, self-disfigured and hopelessly embruited race, ever lured from the remote, unexplored and dreadful interior wilds ...

So they keep the cage ready. Keep the old posters and handbills. Like they keep my handbill.

KRAO — THE "MISSING LINK"

And I look at the picture of the small hairy ape-woman, wearing nothing but a loin cloth and ornate wrist bands. But it is not really me. Look at my face. I am surely not really that hairy. And my limbs — they are not so ape-like. And listen to my voice. Is this the voice of a missing link? It could pass for any mid-western accent.

I know who I am. And I know that I was not born a missing link. She is the creation of Mr Barnum.

I have been that created creature for many years now, but there are still some nights when I tell my own stories and sing my own songs. Perhaps they are songs from the Laotian jungle. Or perhaps they are songs from a poor mid-western mother, impoverished, who gave birth to an extraordinary rare child, endowed with hair from head to foot.

Is that what I dream, you suspect? Is that my own created world? No. My dream is of a land of monkey-women. Where to be a hairy woman with almond-shaped eyes is considered quite normal. But it is a world where those who capture and display the bodies of beautiful creatures, like foxes and mink, or like the Fijians and the Zulus and the Australians, are considered savages. And these savages are all put on exhibition, for all the monkey-women and boomerang throwers of the world to gaze upon.

And they all shake their heads in amazement, for the very existence of such savages is beyond any world they have ever imagined.

Jandamarrajandamarrajandamarra!

The Kimberleys, 1894

It is a dark night in the Kimberleys, the timeless hours between midnight and dawn. Starlight faintly illuminates the many ranges — sharp walls of rock that echo distant nocturnal calls and appear to move slowly closer to a sleeping figure.

Constable Bill Richardson tosses under his blanket. Shivering despite the warm night. The fever is coming back. Creeping up through his bones and beginning to storm furiously in his blood.

He has been out in the field for nearly two months. It is time to go back to Derby, he thinks. Time to bring the prisoners in.

He turns his head and looks out the door of the abandoned homestead. He can see the 16 black tigers are still awake. All sitting in a ring around the large fire. Bound at the neck by a heavy chain. He can hear them chanting over the crackle of the fire.

There will be a promotion for him in this, he knows. Those men are the ring leaders of the Bunuba uprising. Lilamarra, Muckenara, Tulburra. And even the mighty Ellemarra, who has boasted that no white man's bullet could harm him. Ellemarra the invincible, who has said that no white man's chain would ever hold him. He was there too. Sitting in the dust. On the chain. Eyes blazing in the fire's light.

Constable Richardson lays his head back down and feels the tremors run through his body. Wishes he was back in Derby already. Wishes to be rid of the fever. Wishes the wet season had come. Wishes to hell they'd stop chanting, so he could sleep.

They were probably singing to his two black troopers, Pigeon and Captain, he thinks. Calling to them to free them. But he knows he can trust his men. Pigeon won't betray him, he thinks, even though he's a Bunuba man himself. He knows Pigeon is an outcast from his own people. Knows it as he knows it is Pigeon who has really caught the 16 tall strong men out there. Even Ellemarra. As he knows that Pigeon saved his life when one night he ventured too close to the tigers. One black arm shot out. As fast as a snake. Grabbed him. Pulled him into their midst. The chain was quickly around his neck, would have choked him in an instant. But Pigeon and Captain fought them off. Clubbed and beat their own people to free him.

They were good boys, he thought. Loyal. You couldn't get white troopers that loyal.

He knew they'd keep a careful watch on the prisoners all right. And they'd keep an eye on the camp blacks who still hung around the old homestead. They'd make sure that none of them threw a stray nail or small piece of wire to the prisoners. They were adept at picking the locks on the chains.

Richardson listens to the drone of the chant. Maybe they were telling Pigeon and Captain their vain boasts of how they were going to drive the whites from their land. Drive them into the sea off Derby. Spear the cattle and the sheep and spear the white men until the earth ran thick with their blood. Rivers of it, awaiting the fury of the wet season to wash it into the sea.

Richardson tosses again. Shivers. They'll be able to set off in the morning, he thinks. He is sick of Lillimooloora station. Doesn't wish to spend one more night at the ghost homestead.

He recalls the days when he used to work there, as a boundary outrider. The solitary life suited him. Riding the quiet wide spaces between the ranges, listening to the echoes of his shouts off the cliff walls. Spearing the iron-hard earth for fence posts. He could hide from his past in the emptiness of the landscape.

Pigeon had worked on the station too, as a rouseabout. He was hiding from his own troubles. He was a capable boy. He stood out from all the other station blacks. He could ride and shoot better than any young white man he had ever worked with. He was one in ten thousand. But at what cost was it to him, as a

Bunuba black man? Richardson sometimes wondered. He now belonged to neither the blacks nor the whites.

Were the prisoners calling on him to return to them? Singing tribal songs to him? Calling him their brother. Calling him by his tribal name — Jandamarra.

Richardson shivers again. Waits patiently for sleep to come upon him on soft footsteps. He moves his leg and hits his knee on the hard metal of his rifle lying by his side. Kicks it a little further away from him. He closes his eyes tighter and feels the ache in his bones start to recede. Feels himself drifting a little. Somewhere between sleep and waking.

Then he hears nothing. Thinks that the blacks are gone. He looks out the door at the empty space on the ground around the fire. They were there a moment before and now they are gone. He blinks once or twice. It is as if they have melted into the earth.

Then he sees their dark outlines there, lying on the ground. Sleeping. He closes his eyes once more. Or perhaps they were closed the whole time.

He sees Pigeon rise from his blanket. He is standing over the fire. Standing amongst the prisoners where he had been huddled. Then he turns and is looking in the door of the old homestead at him. His eyes fiery in the fire's light. Bright coals. Slowly advancing on him. His Winchester rifle under his arm. He hears the distinct clink of a bullet being put in the chamber. Thinks he hears it echo off the cliffs of the nearby Napier Ranges. Then the rifle is pointed at his head. A single dark eye. Constable Richardson wants to cry out. But he cannot. His blanket is wrapped so tightly around him that he cannot move.

He tosses his head away and waits for the flash and the noise of the shot. But it does not come. He turns his head back and sees that Pigeon is no longer beside him. He is walking across the dry plains towards the ranges, the prisoners following him. Free. He tries to call to them to come back. But they do not hear him. They follow Pigeon to Windjana Gorge, a few miles away. A special place for the Bunuba. There is something in the rocks and the pool there that they hold sacred. He watches them secrete themselves amongst the rocks. Blending into the shadows. Melting into the rock walls. Waiting.

Then the sun rises. Warming the land. And he can see the distant dust cloud of approaching cattle. Hundreds of head. Heading towards the gorge. Richardson knows who it is. Can see the three white men riding around the herd. Can see Fred Edgar sitting on the wagon. He has boasted how he will tame the land. Run stock all across it. Deep into Bunuba territory. He rides with a year's worth of provisions. And guns. With hundreds of rounds of ammunition.

The men skirt around the deserted Lillimooloora station and head straight for Windjana Gorge. The cattle rush in, smelling the water, leaving a broad trail of prints that can be seen from 100 feet up in the air. Pushing greedily for a drink, muddying the waterhole. *Bulumana* the blacks call them — animals with devil horns. The stockmen ride in after them. Beating at the cattle to make a path for themselves, also keen to drink.

And then the shots ring out. The first bullet hits Frank Bourke and sends him falling into the dust. The next hits Oswald Gibbs, mortally wounding him. Richardson watches the blood trickle slowly from Gibbs's wound as he slips from his horse. Sees the waiting warriors pounce on him with sharp spears. Stabbing quickly. Viciously.

But Fred Edgar, at the stockwagon, has not yet entered the gorge. He hears the shots and knows there is trouble. His black stockmen know it too and are already skirting away. Then Edgar sees Pigeon riding out of the gorge towards him, on Gibbs's blood-stained horse. He sees there is murder in his eyes. Edgar jumps to his own horse and wheels it and rides. Pummelling its flanks desperately with his heels. Rides like a man whose life depends upon suddenly acquiring wings. It's a good 20 miles to Lennard River station and safety. He'll do it in an hour if he flies.

But when he looks over his shoulder he sees Pigeon gaining on him. Sees him holding the rifle to his shoulder as he rides. Feels the bullets whip past like angry insects. He lies lower in the saddle and curses the horse to run faster. Run, run, run, he urges. Back across the wide tracks of the cattle. Raising a thin dust cloud anew. Run, run, run.

Richardson feels for a moment that Edgar is not making any progress. That he is galloping frantically, but held to the land. Ride damn you, Edgar urges. Only five miles now. Getting closer to safety. But Pigeon is gaining on him steadily. Edgar wishes his horse could go faster. He wishes he were flying. Wishes for some miracle.

Then he looks back, expecting to see Pigeon almost upon him. But he sees his pursuer's horse stumble, throwing the black man to the ground. Fred Edgar hopes to see him break his bloody neck. He thanks God for the intercession. But he sees Pigeon climb to his feet, a little dazed but unhurt. Then he curses God for sparing the black devil's life. And keeps riding. The station is in sight now. He doesn't look back again until he has ridden into the yard screaming bloody murder and bloody black uprising.

Pigeon, Richardson sees, turns on his heel and begins running back to the gorge. Twenty miles. He eats the distance up quickly. Arrives back at the gorge to find his mob have looted the wagon. Found the food. Found the whisky. Found the guns. Pigeon sets fire to the remains. A thick plume of smoke rises into the late afternoon sky, telling all the tribes what they have done. Telling the whites what they have done. The blacks dance and hoot wildly. Waving spears and guns. Slaughtering some of the cattle to roast on an open fire. Eating them half-cooked, with the blood running down their faces. Screaming out their bloodlust.

And Richardson turns his head back towards the distant town of Derby. Sees that the alarm has been raised there now. Settlers and troopers are assembled in the main street, calling on more men to join them, waving their rifles in the air. Shouting out that the blacks have risen up, that it is war. That they need to be suppressed, quickly and viciously. By the light of a large fire they dance and whip up their bloodlust.

Constable Richardson shakes. It is the fever again. Gripping him tightly once more. Making him quiver as would the deep fear which is the white settlers' unspoken nightmare.

A nightmare of the wild blacks creeping down out of the ranges and sneaking up on them in their beds. Sharp spears piercing their bodies. Quickly. Viciously. Blood spilling out into the dry earth. Shivering in their beds at the mere thought of it.

Now he watches the white patrol riding out of Derby. Follows it across the plains as it approaches Windjana Gorge. Guns loaded. Hungry for slaughter. Sees Pigeon and his men and women melting back into the shadows. Hiding in the caves in the rock walls. Waiting patiently. Knowing the troopers are coming. Ready for them.

By the time the troopers reach the gorge their bloodlust has been tinged with caution. Felix Edgar, Fred's own brother, holds the men back. They see the remains of the wagon and grow silent. If Pigeon is leading the uprising, as Edgar has told them, then they had best be careful. He has learned white men's tactics, knows all about ambushes, knows all about guns. Knows when to be cautious and when to be ruthless.

They send their own blacks up on to the top of the cliffs, to climb down from above. To scout out for the wild blacks. Then they ride into the gorge carefully, keeping cover in sight, unsure if the wild blacks have them in their gun sights or not.

Richardson watches them sitting on their horses. Watches Pigeon watching them. Watches the stillness of the gorge. Thousands of years seem to pass. Then rifles bark. The white men leap for cover. Look about them. Their own blacks have seen the rebels hiding in the shadows and have fired on them. The ambush is foiled. The troopers begin firing lead into the rock walls. Looking for the warriors. They can't see them, but can see the rifle flashes from the cave mouths.

The battle rages all day. The troopers know the blacks are trying to goad them into a charge. But they will not. They whittle the blacks down slowly. Ricocheting bullets off the cave walls. Hearing the screams and moans of the wounded, satisfied by their cries of pain. But neither side can press an advantage.

Then the battle suddenly turns. Ellemarra, the mighty Ellemarra, makes a sudden break from cover and Felix Edgar fires at him, quickly, viciously. Hits him low in the back with a wire cartridge. Watches him slam against the rock face and fall behind the rocks. Hears his screech of pain. Then the wail from the other blacks.

Invincible was he? Immune to white men's bullets was he? Not any more he wasn't. With one of their leaders gone they'd go into disarray. They had them now. They'd seen it before. Now they could charge the blacks' positions and cut them down.

But then Richardson sees Pigeon climb atop a boulder. His rifle at his shoulder. Firing rapidly down on the white men as they emerge from cover. Pinning them down. And his people start fleeing into the darkness of the caves.

Then he sees the troopers start returning the fire. Over and over and over. And he sees the bullets strike Pigeon. One hits him in the shoulder. Then the stomach. Then the chest. Richardson sees him stagger back against the cave entrance. Sees the look of glee on the troopers' faces. They've got him now, they think. The black bastard! They advance across the gorge, still firing. And not even one spear is raised against them. With Pigeon dead too they've lost all fight.

Then they're upon them. But Pigeon is gone! All the blacks are gone. There is only a pool of blood where Pigeon had stood and defied them. And a large bloody handprint on the rock, as if left to taunt them.

The troopers stand there dumbstruck. It is as if Pigeon has disappeared into the rock. They stand there and watch the blood at their feet slowly seeping into the earth.

The troopers linger around the area for some days, but there is no sign of the black warriors, and the troopers know these caves go through the ranges for miles. They don't dare venture into them. They catch some stragglers though. Women and children. They jostle them and frighten them a little. And they all tell the same story. Pigeon is dead!

Then the low heavy clouds of the wet descend upon them, sending torrents of water down upon the land. Forcing the troopers back to Derby, where they sit in their small homesteads, and tell each other that Pigeon is dead. Retell over an open bottle how the three bullets had struck him. All taking claim for those shots. They tell how he died. How he fell to the earth. Regretted that they had not cut his head off and brought it back as a trophy, a warning to other blacks. Then they open another bottle and wait for the wet to pass. They tell how they will drive a thousand head of cattle through the ranges during the dry. Right into the heart of Bunuba territory.

Constable Richardson tries once again to throw his blanket off. The dream is suffocating. He is unable to cast it from him. It is heavy upon him like the earth mantle of a grave. Holding him tightly. He looks out and now sees Pigeon lying in a cave beneath the earth. Being tended to by his mother. His mother the earth. Bathing him in subterranean rivers. Feeding him on shrubs and serpents. Packing poultices of plants and mud into his wounds as his blood seeps into the earth where he lies. And slowly he is reborn of the earth. A part of the ranges. A part of his homeland.

And Richardson sees Pigeon rise up from his subterranean haven. Healed. Reborn. No longer Pigeon. No longer a white mans' black. He is now Jandamarra! Warrior leader of the Bunuba. As tall as the ranges. And the warriors and women follow him down onto the plains where they steal into the nightmares of the settlers.

Days pass. At last the dry returns. And Richardson sees the men in Derby have begun to hear the whispers of rumours, as faint, yet persistent, as the last drips of water falling from the eaves of their homesteads. Cattle have been speared. Provisions stolen. A distinct footprint sighted. And a name is whispered over and over and over. Jandamarrajandamarrajandamarra!

The troopers return to the field. But they are unable to catch more than a glimpse of Jandamarra's footprints. He continues spearing cattle and raiding stations. And he continues to elude all efforts to capture him. Those blacks they do capture tell unsettling stories. They say Jandamarra has been reborn as some kind of magic man. They say that his soul lies deep in the earth by a pool in some cave and that his body is free to roam the country, invincible to their bullets. They say that he can turn into a bird and fly. They say he can disappear like a ghost. They say he is going to lead the Bunuba warriors to slay the whites. To push them all back into the sea where they came from.

It takes some weeks for the dispirited troopers to work themselves back up into a bloodlust again. It takes many bottles and offers of promotion or threats of dismissal before they can muster a large party to deal with Jandamarra once and for all. Armed with their rifles and outrage, they ride to Windjana Gorge, scout around it, and then settle into the deserted Lillimooloora station, using it for their base to scour the surrounding ranges. But they are on Jandamarra's land now. He lives in the ranges. And Constable Richardson sees him grow up from the ground. Rise up from the limestone. As tall as the ranges. One hundred feet high. He can reach down to Lillimooloora. Reach down and grab the troopers there. They toss fitfully in their sleep, shivering despite the night's warmth. A fever to bring nightmares. Nightmares of the blacks rising up from atop the ranges. Hurling spears down upon them. Quick and vicious. And there, leading them, is Jandamarra. His rifle aimed at them. A dark eye trained on them.

The troopers awaken very weary, the shadows of the ranges still upon them. It has been a restless night. They do not like Lillimooloora station. They do not want to spend another night here. They send the black troopers outside to scout around, but they rush back in quickly. Somebody has broken into the store, they say. Somebody has plundered their provisions, they say. Somebody has sprinkled flour on the ground outside the homestead and left clear footprints in it. They look at the prints and know them well. The blacks can read them like a name. Jandamarrajandamarrajandamarra, they whisper. He has been here. The troopers nearly shit themselves. The thought of Jandamarra standing in the doorway, with a Winchester rifle aimed at their sleeping heads causes them to shake at the knees. They retreat further into the abandoned homestead, peering out at the ranges.

Richardson watches the day becomes night becomes days becomes nights. Sees how Jandamarra besieges the troopers. Visits the homestead by night. Disappears into the ranges during the day. He is in the caves. He is the caves. Filling the tunnels and the rocks walls. Merging into them. Gaining strength from them. And at night he boldly stalks around the homestead. He throws rocks onto the roof, keeping the troopers awake. Slowly wearing them down. Lets them know this is Jandamarra's land. Until one morning they mount their horses and flee back to Derby.

Now Jandamarra ventures down to the plains, crossing the land freely. He slays those who venture into his territory, driving livestock or looking vainly for gold. He spears cattle. Slaughters sheep. Keeps back the vast herds that press upon Bunuba land.

But the settlers and troopers will not be beaten back entirely. Richardson watches punitive expeditions ride out time and time again. Attacking black camps. Shooting women and children. He sees the waterholes run red with blood as they regain their confidence. Reach back into Jandamarra's territory.

Then Richardson sees Jandamarra on horseback again. Sees him galloping across the plains. The horse throws up clouds of dust. Richardson thinks it is like watching him from way up on a tall cliff. Or from the sky. Looking down on the unchanged landscape. The land is so vast. Even Jandamarra is so small, he thinks. He is galloping hard, but he doesn't seem to be making any headway.

And then Richardson has a sudden thought — a dream revelation — that Jandamarra, in his physical form, is only temporal. As a person, as a man, he cannot keep the whites off his land forever. But if he were something other than a man? Then the notion passes and he sees the troopers chasing Jandamarra. A large band of them. They have caught five prisoners. Have them on a chain further back. Like the 16 men Richardson remembers he once held. Many are the same men, he sees.

But this patrol is different from the others Jandamarra has fought. Not only have they caught many of the Bunuba warriors, but they are tracking Jandamarra himself.

Richardson sees why. The patrol is following a black trooper. The whites call him Micki. They urge him on as he rides faster than them, as if he had wings. Easily outstripping them, gaining on Jandamarra.

And he sees there is fear in Jandamarra's eyes for the first time. Richardson imagines that Jandamarra sees this black trooper as something else. A magic man like himself. *Jarlnggangurru*, the blacks called it.

He watches Micki shooting from the saddle. Just as Jandamarra had done. Sees Jandamarra's horse go down. Sees Jandamarra within reach of the ranges. Within reach of safety of the dark crevices there. Running towards them. Running on the spot. Sees him look to the ranges. Look back to the rapidly approaching black trooper. Sees him raise his own rifle as they both fire. Sees the bullets fly wildly as the two men duck and weave. Shooting and running amongst the rocks. He sees Jandamarra fall to the dirt. Hit.

Micki has him. But the white troopers are now upon them, galloping hard. Not wishing to miss the death blow. Wishing to administer it themselves. They tell Micki to step back. One of the troopers strides over to Jandamarra and levels his rifle at his head. Tightens his finger on the trigger. But Jandamarra suddenly opens his eyes. Lifts his own rifle and fires. The trooper falls back wounded. But Jandamarra has been hit again too.

The troopers rush to their comrade while Jandamarra leaps into the tall grass. Crawls to the safety of the rocks nearby. The troopers hunt for him, but can only find bloodstains. They retreat to their camp where their prisoners are. Tend their wounds. Tell each other how they nearly had him. Send out Micki and a patrol to catch him. Settle down for the night. They sleep fitfully, shivering in their blankets despite the night's warmth.

Constable Richardson can see what will happen. He tries to call out. But his call echoes faintly off the walls of the nearby ranges like a nocturnal call of the land.

At first light a trooper stands up. A shot rings out. He falls dead. Then their horses are freed and bolt in all directions.

The troopers huddle together. The black prisoners on the chain are grinning. Whispering the name over and over. Jandamarrajandamarrajandamarra.

The troopers are scared now. Really scared. They are on open ground. Jandamarra is on one side of them. Firing on them. Then on the other side. Rising from the dry earth, firing on them and then sinking back into the earth again. Then he is on a new side, firing at them. Then on two sides at once. Then all around them. There is abject terror in the troopers' eyes. Jandamarra is legion, for he is many.

Then the desperate troopers grab the black prisoners and herd them into a circle. They hide behind the darkness of their bodies. They are safe now, they think. Jandamarra will not shoot his own people. And they fire back into the wide grassy plain. Praying for a change of luck.

And change it does. As furious and inevitable as the approaching wet season. The other patrol returns to the sound of the battle. Micki is quickly off his horse and is tracking Jandamarra. Following the bloodstains as if they were broad footprints. So broad he could see them even if he were 100 feet up in the air.

Micki tracks Jandamarra back towards the ranges. He is heading back towards his subterranean sanctuary. Where the blacks say his spirit lives.

For three days Micki tracks Jandamarra over the hot and jagged limestone rocks of the ranges. For three days Jandamarra evades him. Edging ever closer to safety. But when he reaches the mouth of his secret cave Micki is standing there. Waiting for him. As patient as the landscape.

And Richardson watches Jandamarra stand up atop the range. Rising up from the limestone. A hundred feet tall. Micki fires just once. The shot echoes loudly off the cliff walls. Seems to echo forever. The bullet hits Jandamarra. He falls. Over and over and over. Growing smaller as he tumbles to the ground. He hits the earth hard. His body smashing on the hard rocks of his own land.

And Micki just stands there. Richardson sees his dark face shows nothing. Then the troopers ride up to the body of Jandamarra. They are grinning like they have found gold. They cut off his head. They will make a quid or two out of this, they think. They will drink and dine on this for many a night.

'We've got the bugger now, eh?' says one of the troopers to Micki.

But Micki doesn't answer. He is looking up at Jandamarra. Not the body. He sees him in the land. Filling the tunnels and caves of the ranges. As broad and as strong as the peaks before them.

Micki turns and rides away. Knows that he has not won anything. Knows that he will be dead soon, before he ever returns to his own land. Knows that the white men will be drunk at Lillimooloora station that night. Knows they will now be dreaming of the thousands of head of cattle they will send through the ranges to graze on Bunuba land. But he knows that Jandamarra's spirit still lives in that land. Will never be defeated now.

Constable Richardson shivers again. Hears the clink of metal upon metal. Like the sound of the black prisoners easing the chain off the welts on their necks. Or the sound of a rifle being cocked. He opens his eyes and looks up. It is Pigeon. Leaning over him.

Richardson tries to toss his blanket off. Tries to shake the dream and tries to hold onto it as well. He wants to tell Pigeon about it. Wants to tell him what he has seen. His vision clears. And he sees it is not Pigeon. He knows it is Jandamarra standing over him. A hundred feet tall. The rifle pointed at his head. A single dark, menacing eye.

Constable Richardson doesn't even have time to call his name before the rifle explodes in his face.

The shot echoes loudly off the nearby Napier ranges. Echoes forever.

The Last Battle

Archangel, 1918

A shell explodes overhead. As bright as a star. It startles Private O'Connor awake. His eyes snap open wide. Staring around quickly, he sees the snow and icy mud of the trench. Sees Private Duigan staring at him like he's been staring at him forever, his dark face hidden in the late afternoon's gloom. Just the whites of two eyes regarding him.

Private O'Connor closes his eyes again. Holds his hands over his face, as if shutting out the world around him.

'Jesus,' he says softly. 'I was dreaming I was back at Gallipoli.'

Private Duigan smiles and shakes his head slowly. 'I'm not keepin' you 'ere am I?' he says. 'You can go back any time you wanna.'

Bloody Abo! thinks Private O'Connor. He was starting to drive him crazy. Wasn't a man you could talk to. Not like one of his mates. Not like Mick had been. This bloke was always goading him. Always taking his words and turning them around and around until they meant something different from what he'd said.

He turns and peers over the edge of the shell hole they are sheltering in. Tries to see what is happening over in the Russian lines. There is some movement there, but it is too far away. And his eyes are done.

He slumps back and tries not to look at Duigan. He wishes he was bloody-well done of him. Wishes he was done of the whole bloody thing. The war had been over six weeks already and here they were in Russia. Fighting the bloody Bolsheviks. Or trying to. With no supplies, no reinforcements, no food. Nothing.

He'd been stuck in this shell hole for three days with Duigan. Sitting side by side, shivering in the cold, starving, crapping and pissing in the frost. Waiting for something to happen.

He looks across at Duigan again. He's still staring at him. Like he's going to be his next feed or something. They'd fuck-all food left. Fuck-all water. And fuck-all interest in the war any more.

'Fuckin' war,' mutters O'Connor.

'Anyway, what's Gallipoli got that this place 'asn't got?' asks Duigan.

Sarcastic bastard! 'At least it was warm,' says Private O'Connor. 'Warmer than it'll ever get here in this fucking place. What's it called again?'

'Archangel,' says Duigan.

Private O'Connor snorts. 'Sounds like something from Christmas. Which must be any bloody day now.'

'Tomorrow,' says Duigan. 'But that's good, eh — didn't they ever tell you the war would be over by Christmas?'

'Happy fucking Christmas then,' says O'Connor and closes his eyes. He doesn't want to talk to him any more. It's like being in a trench with a bloody Bolshie. He was always going on about how the Russians are entitled to defend their own land. How they were invaded. Always going on about war and land. About the Turks at Gallipoli. The Russians in Russia. And about the bloody Battle for Bathurst! That was stupid. They'd fought over that.

He'd been telling Duigan about his ancestors. How his great-grandfather had fought at the Battle of Waterloo, under Wellington, and Duigan reckoned that his grandfather had fought at the Battle of Bathurst under General Windradyne.

Of course he told him that it was bullshit. There was no such battle.

'Just cause you never 'eard of it, just cause it ain't written in any history books, don't mean it didn't 'appen,' Duigan said. And he reckoned that General Windradyne and his Wiradjuri tribe had fought the soldiers to a standstill around Bathurst for two years. He went on and on about it. All the names of the blackfellas who had been killed. Where they were shot or wounded. Like he'd read and memorised every bloody detail of it in some bloody book.

'It was a real battle that really happened,' Duigan had said, not like this one they were fighting now.

'What do you mean?' O'Connor had asked him.

''Aven't you 'eard? The 'igh Command is denying our existence. Saying they never sent troops against the Bolsheviks. 'Ad nothing to do with this mess.'

Private O'Connor looks away from him. Lifts his head slightly over the edge of the crater. Suddenly nervous. As if looking for another hole to crawl to. Another person to huddle beneath the bullets with. Then he looks back at Private Duigan, who says to him, 'Better keep your lid down. The Bolshies seem to be getting ready for another assault.'

Now Private O'Connor really is worried. 'How many bullets you got left?' he asks. Although he doesn't really need to ask again.

'Three. You?'

'Two.' Neither man needs to look into the breach of his gun to confirm it. They've been counting the bullets over and over like they had counted the few remaining tins of food.

Private O'Connor isn't even sure his frozen fingers will be able to work his rifle any more if he needs to fire it. The frost is too deep in his bones.

'Christ!' says Private O'Connor. Wishes he really was at Gallipoli again. It was horrific — blood and dust and flies and diarrhoea and bullets and everything — but it wasn't anything as bad as this. And he had mates with him there. Like Mick. And when you had mates you could laugh away the fear. Talk it out of you.

'Can you see anything over there?' he asks. 'You blackfellas are supposed to have pretty good eyesight. Mine's buggered. All this snow.'

Private Duigan doesn't even raise his head. 'I can see they're going to overrun us if they attack again.'

Private O'Connor reaches into his tunic and pulls out a small notebook. Bent and worn. He opens it and grasping a small pencil painfully in his shaking fingers he begins writing.

Private Duigan watches him for a moment. Like he watches him each time he writes and asks the same question again. 'Tell it like it really 'appened, eh?'

Private O'Connor doesn't say anything for a moment. Then, 'I'm recording this for history.' He huddles closer over his small book. The letters are awkward and ill-formed. He doesn't really know what to write. More about the snow and pain and cold and despair. But he doesn't want to talk to Private Duigan. Is sick of him. Sick of the cold. Sick of the war. Sick to his stomach. Sick of everything.

He wishes he was with his old mate Mick again, even here in this frozen hell hole. They went through most of the war together. Best mates. In thick and thin. Laughing at danger and death whenever it crept up inside them. And just before the end he was killed. A falling bloody bullet of all things. Minding his own business, miles from the front and a bullet falls smack on his head. Dead. Just like that. Fired from his own side they reckoned.

The pencil falls from his fingers. He tries to pick it up again, but his fingers won't work. He keeps trying. Finally picks it up and just holds it.

'What good you reckon them words are?' Duigan asks. 'They won't turn back a single bullet.'

'I've got to write it like it happened,' says O'Connor. 'Someone has to write it.'

'Yeah. Gotta write up 'istory just as it 'appened.'

O'Connor grits his teeth. Bloody Abo! Wishes he'd never told him that he was planning to be a history teacher before the war came along. He'd recited to Duigan the list of English kings and queens going back five centuries.

Then Duigan says, "'Ere, why don't you write that we invade the Russians' land and they lay down their arms and let us take it without a fight? Then it will become the truth, eh?'

O'Connor doesn't even look at him. Bastard! He closes the book and closes his eyes again. Wishes he were back in the dream of Gallipoli. Fighting with Mick. Laughing away the cold and frost and hunger and fear and sickness and everything.

He opens his eyes and looks at Private Duigan. Stares at him staring back at him, the whites of his eyes bright in the gloom. He wants to tell him to fuck off, to go and find another crater to hide in. But he asks, 'How does a blackfella end up here fighting Russians?'

"'Ow does a whitefella?' he asks him back.

'I was volunteered. This or gaol.'

'What charge?'

'Mutiny. Refused to go up the line in France. A whole battalion of us.'

'I never 'eard about that,' says Private Duigan.

'Nuh. It didn't exist either. And what about you?'

'Same thing. Avoiding prison.'

'Where?'

'Near Cowra.'

'Cowra? On what charge?'

'Being black. The family is still there. They call it a reserve. But it's a prison camp. You can't do anything there. Can't get a job. Can't visit your relatives. Can't go to your own land. Can't do anything at all without a permit.'

Private O'Connor looks at him. Carefully. Studies the white eyes in the dark hidden face. 'Bullshit!' he says.

Private Duigan only shrugs. 'You're right. If it's not in a 'istory book it never 'appened.'

'But you're not even a full blackfella. Look at your skin.'

'It's black enough to prevent me from getting a drink in a pub. Black enough to prevent me getting citizenship. But white enough when they want me to join the army.'

'Then why did you do it?'

'Why did you?'

Private O'Connor shrugs. 'I dunno.' Then, despite himself, he keeps talking. Feels the fear growing out of him. Just a little. 'I thought I used to know, like when the war started and all, y'remember what it was like? You just had to be in it. Defend the empire and all that. Y'know?'

Private Duigan shakes his head slowly. 'No. I don't know.'

'Well then why the fuck are you fighting?'

'Seems to me like I've been fightin' so long I don't remember why any more. But my people've been fightin' forever, eh? After this it'll just be somethin' else.'

O'Connor doesn't know what to say. So he turns and looks over the edge of the shell hole. Keeps his head low. Watches the movement in the distance.

'They're up to something,' he says.

'What'll ya do if those Bolshies overrun us?' Duigan asks. 'They might get your book and write in it. What do you reckon they'll say? That we fought and died valiantly? That we were stupid enough to have volunteered for a job we didn't want to do? That we were poorly led and abandoned in the field?'

'Have a look over the top,' says O'Connor, ignoring him again. 'Tell me what you can see?'

'Oright,' says Private Duigan, making a great effort of rolling over onto his stomach and carefully lifting his head to peer out across the frosty landscape. 'I can see the past,' he says, 'And it isn't anything I ever want to go back to.'

'What can you see?' Private O'Connor asks louder. He wishes again that he wasn't in this shallow trench with this smart-arsed blackfella who keeps turning his words back on him. Thinks of Mick again. Feels the cold chill of fear creeping into his guts again.

'I think they're gettin' ready to charge,' says Duigan softly.

'Fuck!' says O'Connor. The fear is so cold within him now he is shivering. He reaches down to the frozen mud, rubs some in his hands until it thaws a little, and then smears it over his face. Colour of the earth.

'Where your people from?' Private Duigan asks. 'You suddenly look familiar. Maybe we're related.'

THE LAST BATTLE

O'Connor is about to tell him, then realises Duigan is making fun of him. Again. And then he knows he can't tell him anyway. It was his ancestors who had cleared the land around the Bathurst area. About 100 years ago, during the reign of King George III. During his insane years. Cleared the trees and cleared the blacks. Shot at them. Pinned them down and shot them. Like the Russkies had them pinned down. He was right. When you thought about it, it was a war. But how did you tell a fella that that's what your ancestors did to his ancestors? Even a pain-in-the-arse Abo like Duigan?

'Ireland and England mostly,' says Private O'Connor.

'No Russian blood?'

'No!'

'Pity, eh?'

And despite himself, O'Connor almost laughs.

Duigan turns onto his belly again and looks over the rim of the shell hole. Says, 'D'y'know who'd I'd like to see chargin' over the field? All the whitefella generals and politicians who put us 'ere.'

'Yeah,' says O'Connor and smiles now. 'I'd sure as shit like to see them leading a charge against the Russkies.'

'No,' says Duigan. 'No. I want to see them runnin' at us. Right into my gun sights.'

'What's your problem?' asks O'Connor. Shakes his head a little. Works his rifle bolt back and forward slowly. Keeps it moving. Gotta stop it freezing. 'You sure you know which side you want to fight for?'

'I think I can recognise the enemy all right,' Duigan says.

'You Abos have got a hell of a chip on your shoulder,' O'Connor says. 'And anyway, what makes you think the generals and politicians will desert us here? Deny we were ever sent here?'

'Why not?' asks Private Duigan. 'Now the war's over they've got political careers to think of. Lots of promises to break. Lots of people to tread on. We'll just be unknown soldiers, lost in action.'

'It's not always like that,' says Private O'Connor.

'Always 'as been as far I can remember — and I seem to remember back at least a few 'undred years.'

'Well I reckon that sometimes you blackfellas write your own history to suit yourselves too,' says Private O'Connor.

And Private Duigan smiles. Those white teeth in the darkness. 'Maybe we do,' he says. 'So maybe we 'ave more in common than we realise.' And he reaches into his jacket, pulls out some tobacco and papers, makes a thin little cigarette, lights it and passes it across to O'Connor.

Private O'Connor looks at it a moment. Then takes it. Inhales it deeply. Feels the smoke warming his lungs. Filling him with hope and something more he can't describe. Something like wanting to reach out and shake Duigan by the hand. Really grasp him tightly. Laugh and tell him that he's a miserable pessimistic bastard, but that if the generals and politicians would only stick their heads up high enough they'd both knock 'em all off. Both of 'em would. And he clings to that feeling like it is the only true thing left in the world. Their only way out of this mess.

But before he can say a word there is a distant faint whistle and the nearer rattle of a machine-gun.

'Shit!' says Private O'Connor. And draws a sharp breath. 'It's on!'

Private Duigan lifts his head a little, then drops back down in the shell hole. Reaches into his jacket and begins rolling another thin cigarette. He looks sideways at Private O'Connor and smiles. Bright enough to read by.

'Save your bullets,' he says. 'Get out ya little book and write in that instead. But you'll need to be quick.'

'Write what?' asks O'Connor.

'Write our future, eh?'

Mrs Shackleton's Freezer

England, 1919

Mrs Shackleton is in her kitchen, determinedly trying to defrost the freezer. Ice has grown thick around the inner walls, encompassing the shelves, and preventing the door from closing properly.

She has a sharp knife in her hand and is hacking at the ice. Chips fly up and sting her face. The chill air makes breathing difficult. But she perseveres.

'We found ourselves caught in the grip of the ice,' calls out her husband, Ernest, from the next room. 'What do you think of that, dear?'

'That's fine,' she calls back, still stabbing madly at the ice.

He is seated in front of the fire, in the living room, writing his memoirs.

'Two long years adrift on the pack ice,' he calls out.

'Sixteen months,' she corrects him. And much of that was spent on board the ship *Endurance*, she thinks. Before he lost it. He could be terribly absent-minded at times, and would lose anything.

She shifts position on the floor to get a better angle of attack. The ice has grown hard and colourless. It has the texture of rock.

Sir Ernest considers the words he has written before him and thinks about striking them out. But they are set there now. Dark tracks across the empty whiteness of the page. Showing his progress like staggering footprints.

The first steps were always the most difficult, he thinks. Overcoming the sheer emptiness in front of him. He leans back in his chair and sighs, rubbing his eyes with his knuckles. This writing business is immensely harder than he had imagined. He has been sitting here for hours. His back is sore and his hands are cramped, as if they were frostbitten. But he won't give in. He has to tell the story this time, tell what really happened.

Mrs Shackleton is down on her knees. Contemplating the darkened interior of the freezer. He'd insisted upon roast beef again for dinner. His favourite. But prices were going up. Antarctic explorer's pensions weren't what they used to be. One had to struggle a bit more to make ends meet.

'Each day was a fight against the ice for survival,' he says aloud. 'We hunted seals for food and fuel. We even ate our dogs.'

Dog meat would be cheaper than roast beef, Mrs Shackleton thinks. I wonder if he'd notice?

He has written half a page now. More descriptions of the ice. Then he tells how they sailed south from Europe in 1914, leaving Britain in the early grip of war. In the icepacks of the Weddell Sea, beyond the Antarctic Circle, they became stuck in their own terrible conflict. The pack ice seized their ship and held them fast.

Words tell the story, but there is a lot they don't tell, he thinks. He has re-read his journals, and those of his party, but knows there was something more to it all that none of them has quite captured.

So he holds up the photographs again. There is one in particular. He looks at the figure of the man in it. Who was that man? It is entitled 'Ernest Shackleton' and it shows himself as a younger man. But it seems to him that it's not a person he can remember. The bearing is heroic. Arms folded confidently. Face grim and epic. Yet the whole picture is surrounded by darkness. That's it, he thinks. That's what he's trying to capture in his telling. That darkness.

Mrs Shackleton chips around the edges of the ice. Testing its strength. Peering into the depth. There is no light deep within the freezer. She can just make out the distant shape of the roast.

'That Frank Hurley chap really knew his craft,' Sir Ernest calls out. Mrs Shackleton knows his work well. His photographs of the ship *Endurance* hang all around the house. There is one over the fireplace showing the vessel surrounded by ice. And behind the *Endurance*, pressing closely upon the ship, is a towering iceberg, many times larger than the ship. Dwarfing it with its enormity. And within the iceberg is a dark shadow.

The darkness is larger than the ship, Sir Ernest thinks, looking at it carefully. Frank Hurley had seen it and had captured it.

'Do you know where he was when I recruited that Hurley chap?' Sir Ernest shouts.

'Yes dear,' says his wife. She has heard the story many times. He was in the outback of Australia, filming the blacks. Primitive wild men with darkened faces.

'He was a singularly driven man,' Sir Ernest says. 'Do you know when I gave the order to abandon ship, he went back and dived into the frozen water of the half-sunken hull to retrieve his films?'

Mrs Shackleton wonders if Mr Hurley ever photographed the interior of a kitchen freezer. Wonders if he could really capture one on film.

'And when we were adrift on the sea in our small lifeboats and had to jettison material to lighten the load, he threw out his rations to keep his films,' he says.

Sir Ernest remembers looking at those negatives of the pack ice. All black on the plates. Darkness. They revealed the truth more fully than the final prints did.

Sir Ernest has started writing again. He tries to describe how they hibernated that first winter, snuggled up inside the ship, barely 390 miles from their destination.

'*We could hear the screams of the gales and the terrible groans of the pressure-tortured ice around us*,' he writes.

Mrs Shackleton puts the knife in between the edge of the freezer and the ice. Tries to force it in. Hears the slow scrape as it moves in, then stops. It starts to bend. She tries to remove it, but it is caught fast.

Sir Ernest rubs his tired bones and massages his fingers. He does not give in easily, he knows that. But the words are not coming. He takes up another photo of Hurley's. It is the most heroic of all, he thinks. It shows the *Endurance* on mid-winter's day in 1914. It is taken at midday, but the sky is totally dark. The ship, illuminated by torchlight and flash, is covered in ice. It looks like a brilliant white sculpture, lifted clear of the ice and sitting atop the floe. It shows a ghost image of their vessel. Spars and ropes gleam white, and pressing in closely all around — the darkness.

He ponders how to capture the image in words. And how to contrast that with the loss of the ship.

He picks up the next photo. It shows their proud ship crushed and listing badly, half submerged beneath the ice. Perhaps this is where he should start, he thinks. At the point of disaster. He tries to bring back the terrible feeling of dread that filled them all.

But he writes: '*The position was latitude 69°19'S, longitude 50°40'W.*'

He looks at the words and ponders them.

Mrs Shackleton is working on the knife and can feel it coming loose.

Sir Ernest rubs his cramped fingers and forces the pen across the page once more.

Just before leaving, I looked down the engine room skylight as I stood on the quivering deck and saw the engines dropping sideways as the stays and bed-plates gave way. I cannot describe the impression of relentless destruction that was forced upon me as I looked down and around. The floes, with the force of millions of tons of moving ice behind them, were simply annihilating the ship.

'We took to the ice,' he calls to his wife. 'Tried unsuccessfully to cross it, and then set up tents. We lived on the drifting ice.'

'Yes dear,' says Mrs Shackleton, the knife now back in her hands.

'We were confined to our tents during blizzards, but we made many imaginary journeys. Narrated to each other. The Far East. Burma. And the outback deserts of Australia.'

Sir Ernest remembers those wide, flat hot deserts that were at times almost beyond their imaginations. He looks into the living room fire and remembers Frank Hurley's tales of the dances of the blacks at night. Primitive peoples whose only want in life was food, shelter and ritual.

'So like our own lives,' he says.

'Who?' asks his wife.

'The blacks,' says Sir Ernest. 'Do you know,' he calls, 'Hurley said they underwent great initiation rituals of strength and endurance. Mutilating their bodies. Suffering extremes.'

Mrs Shackleton shakes her head. 'So very alike,' she mutters.

'And they were driven to journey across the land. Walkabout, he called it. But it was more than a journey. It was a way of discovering some spiritual strength within themselves. Imagine how that sounded to us, captive in our tents. Can you imagine that dear?'

Mrs Shackleton doesn't answer straight away. Then she says, 'I'm sure it was difficult at the time to understand what drove them to do it.'

Sir Ernest thinks of the photos he has seen of Frank Hurley and the dancing tribes of black men.

'It must have been difficult for them, after so many years of living in primitive isolation, trying to enter the twentieth century.'

'Who?' his wife asks again, unsure if he is still talking about the Australian Aborigines or is back on his memoirs.

Mrs Shackleton has decided on another method of attack. She is chipping determinedly at the thinnest area of the ice, hacking away at it, chip by chip. Thinks of an image of her husband and his men, all kneeling. Hacking at the ice engulfing the *Endurance* with kitchen knives. Then she thinks of all the wives and girlfriends of the men. Imagines them hacking at it, and wonders if they wouldn't have managed to free the ship.

'And finally the ice began breaking up,' he says. 'And new perils confronted us.' He remembers the nightmares in the winter's darkness that haunted him. Anxiety that the ice under their tents was breaking up. Anxiety that it was bearing down on them to crush them. Anxiety that the killer whales would break through the ice beneath them. Anxiety that they would sink into the chill waters in their sleep. Sealed in their sleeping bags.

Mrs Shackleton's hands are turning numb. She can feel her grip loosening on the knife handle. But she keeps at it, ice chips flying into her eyes as she hacks away determinedly.

Sir Ernest writes:

I decided we should strike out in the boats towards Elephant Island. Reached after the most terrible of travails, to find it was a pitiful rock in the ocean. The first land we had stood upon in 16 months, bare and hardly above the reach of the sea.

There is a Hurley photo of that accursed rock somewhere, he thinks, but he cannot find it.

'But we could not stay on Elephant Island,' he says. 'And I had to make the difficult decision to head north to South Georgia Island, 750 miles away, with the best five sailors. We left behind 22 men, crazed, frostbitten and quite worn out.'

Mrs Shackleton no longer has any feeling in her fingers. Perhaps she should stop and place them under warm water? Or fetch her woollen gloves? But she is too single-minded. She is nearly there now.

'We were men of determined mettle,' he says. 'We walked, sledged, sailed, rowed and crawled our way northwards, to be free of that terrible grip of the ice.'

Mrs Shackleton's knees are starting to ache. She shifts her position again.

Sir Ernest thinks about the narrative he is writing. Thinks about the darkness. About what he is trying to capture. He writes:

The men left behind on Elephant Island lived under the upturned boats for four months. They entertained each other with tales heard once, twice and many times over. And they dreamed of small exotic delights like a crackling fire and roast beef.

He reads it over. It tells the story, but still it does not tell of the darkness.

Mrs Shackleton's arm feels like lead. Her knees are aching. She shifts position yet again. Still hacking at the ice.

'I finally saw the darkness,' Sir Ernest calls out. 'On the voyage to South Georgia. Deep in the night amidst a terrible storm, I was on watch and saw a thin pale line on the horizon. "The weather is breaking!" I called.'

Mrs Shackleton pauses. She has not heard this story before. He writes:

Then a moment later I realised that what I had seen was not a rift in the clouds but the white crest of an enormous wave. During 26 years' experience of the ocean in all its moods I had not encountered a wave so gigantic ... I shouted, 'For God's sake, hold on! It's got us!'

'But we survived,' he calls out. 'We survived and finally reached the safety of South Georgia.'

Mrs Shackleton resumes her attack on the ice. Sir Ernest recalls that the men carried him ashore. All exhausted. He still screaming.

The weary men calmed him. Tried to restore him to his heroic stature. Arms folded. Face grim and epic. But he woke again, at about two in the morning, pointing towards the steep cliff above them, screaming, 'Look out, boys! Look out!'

The mountainous darkness had returned to kill us, he thought.

'But we survived,' he says again. Much softer.

Mrs Shackleton tries to grasp the knife in both hands. Her breath is laboured, sending out streams of mist. She can hear the fire crackling in the next room. She feels the chill of the frost seeping deep into her lungs. But she doesn't slow her assault.

The men nursed me back to health, Sir Ernest recalls. And then sent their leader off to cross the island. To climb over the glaciers that had never before been trodden upon. Vast deserts of rocky ice. To stand upon them heroically.

In his mind he thinks that he wept when he heard the sharp cry of the steam whistle of the whale factory. But he writes:

Never had any one of us heard sweeter music. It was the first sound created by outside human agency that had come to our ears since we left Stromness Bay in 1914. It was a moment hard to describe.

And he remembers staggering into the whaling station. Surprising the men there. The firm clutch of another human hand. Of re-entering civilisation. And the surprised look on the faces of the workers. He appeared from nowhere. A wild primitive with blackened face.

'We escaped from the darkness,' he says. 'Only to find it had preceded us. The world had gone mad.'

He remembers his incredulity. Sitting in the station supervisor's small office and being told the news. Gallipoli. The Somme. The slaughter. Millions killed. For so little gain.

Mrs Shackleton drops the knife to the kitchen floor. Her fingers slipped and she has cut herself. Only a small nick. She squeezes it and sees the blood emerge. Then sucks it and picks up the knife once more.

For a moment Sir Ernest considers abandoning his memoirs as inadequate. How to weigh up the travails of a few against the suffering of so many millions? He considers tearing the sheets of paper into small pieces and letting them fall to the floor beside him. Like so much falling snow.

Then Sir Ernest finds Hurley's last photograph of the wild men on Elephant Island, dancing on the frozen rocks, as the rescue boat approaches. It shows not a hint of the darkness.

'We failed in our mission to reach the Pole,' he calls. 'Defeated by the strength of the ice. We never set one foot on the continent. But neither did we lose a single man.

'We had seen God's frozen fury and His glory, and we had reached the naked soul of man,' he writes.

And then, one final blow, and the large block of ice on the upper freezer shelf falls free. It drops to the floor and slides across the lino.

'It needs a final word. How should I describe it dear?' he asks.

Mrs Shackleton peers deep into the frozen depths of the freezer. There it is. She has uncovered the roast!

'A triumph,' she says.

Pastor Strehlow's Journey to the Land of Death

Central Australia, 1927

Pastor Carl Strehlow lived at Hermannsburg mission in Central Australia. One day he fell very ill with pleurisy in the lungs, which developed into dropsy, causing his limbs to swell up with liquids like a baobab tree. It was the first time he had been seriously ill in his 28 years at the mission. He had come there as a young man to bring the word of God to the Aranda people and had become head man at the mission. By his fiftieth year he was a big, heavily bearded man, and was well loved and respected by the Aranda people.

They regarded him highly both for his fairness in settling disputes and his ability to work hard. He was unlike other missionaries in that he took an interest in their traditional stories, often recording them in his books until late into the night. They told him of the totem spirits and of the ancestor journeys that shaped the land, naming each site and describing what happened at each place. Stories that were maps. Stories that were histories. Stories that defined their spirituality. Stories that defined their relationship to the land.

Pastor Strehlow, swelled with dropsy, prayed to his God for relief, but he was already beyond the help of prayer. He knew he must return to the land of his own people to seek medical assistance. He decided to travel down the Finke River towards Adelaide. Two wagons were loaded with all Pastor Strehlow and his family's possessions. Boxes of books and furniture and bird cages were piled high on the wagons and four horses were hitched to each.

They were seven people in the party. They were Pastor Strehlow, his wife Frieda, his 14-year-old son Theo, three Aboriginal drivers — Titus, Hesekiel and Jakobus — as well as the mission teacher, Mr Heinrich. They set off on their journey on 10 October 1927. The Aranda people at the mission were sad to see their pastor so ill. Sad to see him leaving them. They bade farewell to him and sang a hymn in his honour.

His last words to them were:

*May God bless you all
my friends.*

They travelled alongside the Finke River to a watercourse named Tjamangkura, which was close to the border of the land of the honey ant totem people. They then travelled on to Pmokoputa, which marked the entrance to the Krichauff Ranges. They stopped there for lunch to feed on fresh steaks cooked on hot coals. After lunch they travelled on into Ellery Creek Gorge, where the red sandstone cliffs rose up around them.

They stopped the first night at a large waterhole by the Finke. The name of the place was Rubula. They lit cooking fires and wrapped themselves in blankets against the night's chill, and Pastor Strehlow and his wife retired early to their tent.

The next day they set out early and travelled until mid-morning, when they reached the waterhole at Alitera. A police outstation had once been built there. It was later moved further from the Hermannsburg mission after repeated reports of violence on the natives of the area. Pastor Strehlow had many battles with a policeman name Wurmbrand, demanding he keep away from the mission. He had once accosted the policeman, while he was on a patrol, and told him:

*Release these prisoners
And leave this place!
Don't ever let me catch you
hunting people again
at Hermannsburg.*

They then travelled on. They crossed the Finke River at Alitera and then passed over very rocky ground. This caused great discomfort to Pastor Strehlow as the buggy rocked and jolted. They passed onto smoother ground. Then they met up with Jack Fountain, the old mailman, bringing up his camel train towards the mission. They stopped to talk and he gave them their mail. Jack Fountain saw how sick Pastor Strehlow was. They travelled on. They reached Running Waters, where they stopped for lunch, and to read their mail. They had gone about 30 miles from Hermannsburg.

In the afternoon they travelled to Parkes Pass and just before sundown they left the rock walls of the ranges. They camped that night on the flat desert country, where there was no water. The next day they travelled on slowly. They recrossed the Finke River once more, at a point where it was shallow but several hundred yards wide. On the far side they let the horses drink and refilled their water bags. They then travelled on some more. They crossed dusty ground, raising large red clouds as they went. They reached Henbury station late in the day and camped by the Finke River, just short of the station.

Henbury cattle station had been established in the 1870s, by the two Parke brothers, but had since been sold to a man named Joe Breaden after incurring heavy debts. Pastor Strehlow's party set up camp and cooked their evening meal. Two men came down from the station to visit them. Their names were Bob Buck and Alf Butler. Both men had halfcaste children who had been at Hermannsburg, and they had great respect for Pastor Strehlow. They saw how sick he was but said nothing of it. Instead they talked about the country ahead of them that he would have to travel through. Bob Buck said:

That old van of yours
has a helluva load on it,
and those narrow iron tyres ...
are going to cut into the sand
like knives into runny butter.
You'll have to change your team

after half a day's pulling.
There's no water in the Britannia Sandhills,
and there's about twenty-two miles of them.
Now here's my plan ...
Hook some of our donks to the van.

Pastor Strehlow agreed to the offer and then gave the men tea and biscuits. And before leaving for the night, Bob Buck said:

Just one more thing, Mr Strehlow.
I'm sorry you had to leave Hermannsburg
in such a hurry ...
But I tell you this,
You've done a grand job
at the Mission.
Every white man in the country
will tell you that
if you ask him.

Later Pastor Strehlow said to his wife Frieda:

I have always striven to educate my flock
to walk in what I believed to be
the Christian way of life.
I have far too often thought
that we who call ourselves Christians
were a superior folk
to those who neither pray
nor read the Bible.
But these hard-swearing, hard-drinking bush folk,
living with lubras whom they have not married
are the people who are always ready
to show love towards their neighbours
when it is most needed.

The next day they travelled on. They veered away from the river which wound through low hills ahead of them. They rejoined the river at a waterhole named Takalalama. They crossed the river again, and took a more direct route, away from the river, through the Britannia Sandhills. Rain had fallen heavily that year, bringing new growth to the desert land. The mulga and ironwood trees and spinifex tussocks showed new growth all around them. They camped that night in the sandhills.

They travelled on early the next day. They had a long day's journey to make. By noon they had reached the last large red sandhill before rejoining the Finke River. The party travelled around the sandhill and through a gap in the rocks there. It was called Hells Gates. The travellers and donkeys were glad to rejoin the river and rested from the heat of the day under tall box gum trees. The land here was heavily wooded, and many cattle grazed near the waterhole called Uratanga. However, the cattle had brought many flies, which greatly annoyed the travellers.

After lunch they travelled on, without taking rest, until well after dark. Shortly after eight o'clock the travellers could see the distant lights and fires of the Idracowra station, across the Finke River. The donkeys pulled the wagons across the river flats once more. The name of the station came from Itirkawara, the Aranda name for Chambers Pillar, a sandstone formation about 11 miles north of the station. This was the final resting site of Itirkawara, the mythical gecko lizard who, after a rampage across the land, battling other creation totems, had turned into an 150-feet-high sandstone pillar.

The station manager at Idracowra was named Allan Breaden. He was aged about 70, and was one of the first Finke River pastoral pioneers in the 1870s, when the settlers and their cattle commonly had conflicts with the Aborigines over the land. Many of the Aborigines now worked on the cattle stations in the area. Allan Breaden lived at Idracowra station with his Aboriginal wife Jessie and her various children, including his own son Johnson Breaden. He came down to visit Pastor Strehlow and when he saw how sick he was, and how badly the long day's travel had affected him, he offered him his own house to sleep in.

The next day was a Sunday and Pastor Strehlow was very ill and full of despair. The pain of his illness took his spiritual thoughts towards the agonies endured by Job.

The next day Pastor Strehlow was still very ill and Allan Breaden told him he should stay at Idracowra and await help to reach him. He said he would send riders on to Horse Shoe Bend station, where the overland telegraph ran, and where there was a telephone, to bring help. Pastor Strehlow tried to thank him for all his help, but Allan Breaden replied:

Look, it's nothing what I'm doing.
Everyone in this country would be only too glad
to do the same for you.
I'm only sorry I can't do more.

Pastor Strehlow's suffering now increased greatly and his body had swollen even larger, and sores broke out on his skin. He asked repeatedly for God to have mercy upon him, muttering the words in Aranda:

Kyrie eleison
Christe eleison
Kyrie eleison.

And then a single line from the Lord's Prayer:

Thy will be done.

The next evening, towards dusk, riders arrived from Horse Shoe Bend. They were Mrs Ruby Elliot, one of her Aboriginal stockmen, and one of the riders from Idracowra who had ridden out to fetch help. Mrs Elliot went straight in to Pastor Strehlow and saw how sick he was. Then she told him that he would have to travel on to Horse Shoe Bend so that they could get a car up to meet him. She said they could also talk to a doctor over the phone from there. She said that they should leave straight away, and travel through the night so that the heat of the day would not torment him.

And Pastor Strehlow replied:

But how will you get on, Mrs Elliot?
You've been in the saddle for seven hours already.
You must be tired out.
You need a good night's sleep.

But she only replied:

Never mind about me.

Then she said:

*One of the boys and I
will carry storm lanterns
and ride ahead of the buggy.
All your driver has to do
is follow the lights.*

So they travelled on. It was about 30 miles to Horse Shoe Bend, along the route the mail camels took, crossing the rocky Table Mountains. The travelled by night and soon passed by the land of Death. In this land, according to the Aranda people, Death had first come into the world because of the mischievous actions of the Ntjikantja snake brothers. The land there was taboo and even its secret name was only known to the oldest of the snake totem clansmen. It was so barren that even the gum trees were shrunken and misshapen. Travelling past this land was very painful for Pastor Strehlow, as the wagon jarred heavily over the bare rocky ground, causing him great agony. When the sun rose that day they were still travelling and the heat of the day brought asphyxiating breathlessness to Pastor Strehlow.

Eventually they reached softer ground and then soon rejoined the Finke River once more. They crossed the river three times before reaching Horse Shoe Bend. Pastor Strehlow was taken straight to the hotel there and given a room and put to sleep with a heavy dose of laudanum. Horse Shoe Bend was known as Par' Itirka by the Aranda people, and was named after an ancient swollen gum tree that grew nearby on the Finke River. It was said to be as old as creation times and the land there was associated with stories of devastating summer heat.

The next day was a Thursday and Pastor Strehlow sat in his hotel room as the temperature quickly rose to over 100 degrees Fahrenheit. The hotel was owned by Gus Elliot, who was also one of the first settlers on the Finke River. His exact age was unknown, but most guessed he was in his mid-60s. His wife Ruby was less than half that age.

That afternoon Gus Elliot left to bring up the doctor. Frieda Strehlow, who remained constantly with her sick husband, said:

*The doctor should be here by Saturday,
Everything will be alright after that.*

Pastor Strehlow then asked to talk to Ruby Elliot. When she came he told her:

*Mrs Elliot, I am dying.
I have not many more hours to live.
I know that I am dying,
But my wife does not.
When I am gone it will be hard on her.
Please help her and my son.
I can no longer attend to anything.*

That night Pastor Stolz of the Finke River mission arrived at Horse Shoe Bend. He went to see Pastor Strehlow the next morning and saw how ill he was. Pastor Strehlow asked Pastor Stolz to ensure that the Hermannsburg mission was cared for. That day the temperature rose to over 110 degrees Fahrenheit and the tin roof of the hotel creaked noisily in the heat. Pastor Strehlow suffered terribly all through that day, his breathing growing more and more laboured. Late in the afternoon, his wife began to sing a hymn for him, asking for God's help.

But he replied, knowing that death was very near to him now:

*Don't sing that hymn any more, Frieda,
God doesn't help.*

They were his last words. He slumped back peacefully to meet his maker. All the inhabitants of Horse Shoe Bend loudly lamented his passing.

The next day he was put down into the ground, buried in a coffin made from whisky cases. A wooden cross was erected over the grave and smooth water-worn stones were placed on the grave mound forming the initials CS. The mourners then went to the hotel where the bar was thrown open. Police Constable Macky, who had arrived to authorise the death certificate, said:

That's the first time any of you blokes
have ever drunk to the memory of
a bible-puncher, I'll bet.

And one of the drinkers replied:

Yes, he was a good bloke.

The white mourners drank his health and told grand stories about his life while the Aboriginal mourners sat in their camp all afternoon, talking in low tones, carefully avoiding the dead man's name.

The following day it rained and rained all over the land around Horse Shoe Bend. Rain fell heavily, bringing new life. Rain fell heavily where Pastor Strehlow lay buried. Rain fell heavily upon the land of Death.

Lasseter's Last Dream

Central Australia

Harry Lasseter lies against the rock wall and watches the desert sun set over his empire. He's the richest man in the world. But he's stuffed and he knows it. Long black shadows stretch across the landscape. He watches them carefully. Sees them creep across the desert floor towards his little cranny in the rock face.

That lone mulga tree, way out there on the plain, sprouts sharp-edged shadows like grasping fingers. They stretch out towards him. Reach out to grab him.

He tries to move a little to the side. But he is crippled by exhaustion. Too weak. He's well and truly stuffed. All the riches in the world beneath him and he's too weak to avoid a shadow. It creeps faster now, quickening, and then, like a striking snake, darts out and touches his leg. Despite the desert heat he shivers.

He looks back to the sun. It is starting to disappear now. Half under the horizon. It's that time, when everything changes, when everything is clearer. He rolls his head a little to one side and looks up at the rock face. Waits for that instant. Waits for it to turn to gold. The entire ridge. A mountain of gold!

He has seen it a thousand times. Tens of thousand times. But it never fails to draw his breath. To spellbind him. To renew his dream and reinvigorate him. Then there it is. A sudden sharp brightness that flares right across the rock face. All along the side of his reef. A mountain of gold. It is just for an instant, but in that instant he is gold too.

It's bloody beautiful! He'd cry if he had any tears left. Then it is gone. The sun is down. The reef slowly fades back to cold flat rock. It is that time between day and night now. No sun. No stars. No shadows. Everything is much clearer. He looks at his arms and legs. They are thin sticks. All the flesh melted off them. Seeped into the sand.

Poor bugger me, he says to himself. He looks up at the night sky, to that point where he knows the first star will appear. Right over the mulga tree out there. And then there it is. Bright. Stark against the blackness. It seems to dance. Then the other stars appear, slowly at first, then quickening. Tens, then hundreds, then thousands of them.

He follows the stars like he'd follow a map, or a familiar story. Knows just where the next stars will appear. Tens of thousands of them.

He'd heard that the blacks believed that the spirits of the dead went up to the stars. The milky way was a river of spirits. He wonders where his star would be. In some patch of empty blackness. Far from any other stars.

He looks back to the desert. Something is moving out there. Is it the kaditcha man again? He looks towards the mulga tree. He can see its dark outline still there. But there is something further to the south. Now he can see two large bright eyes out there. And he hears a low rumbling growl. Moving towards him. The eyes flash across him. Blinding him. The growl grows louder. Closer now. Then almost deafening. It stops in front of him, with a loud hiss. The doors spring open and a small crowd jumps out.

'You've missed it, you silly bastards,' Harry Lasseter yells. But they don't hear him. A few lift their cameras and fire off flash shots at the rock wall. Another walks a few easy paces away and pisses into the desert sand. Then they leap back onto the bus and drive away. Going flat out. Tape player blaring. Within a few minutes they're gone. No movement. No sound.

'Fucking tourists!' says Lasseter. He hates them. And he remembers the difficulty they had with their own six-wheeled Thornley truck. Constantly digging it out of soft sand. Repairing punctured tyres up to ten times a day. And the heat of the engine igniting the desert grasses under it as they drove.

The landscape finally defeated it. They had to turn back towards Alice Springs. But he pressed on alone. With his camels.

They were going to send support in the aeroplane. The *Golden Quest*. And he remembers that distant single plane ride he once had. Cruising low over the desert, following the contours of the land. Viewing the landscape from the air. How different it looked. So easy to conquer. So easy. From up there he could see his long slow journey like a map. Like a picture. Could see his faint footsteps in the sand as he struggled from waterhole to waterhole, heading onwards alone towards the reef.

But it was so different to be trudging down there, slow heavy step by slow heavy step, across the soft desert sands. Half blind from sand blight, starving and weakened by lack of food. And always having to beware of the blacks. They were always out there. They helped him for a time. Took him into their tribe. Fed him. But grudgingly. And when they smelt the scent of death about him they left him to die.

Una pika purlka. They said. *Kuna kuna*.

He tried to talk with them. Tried to learn their words. Tried to teach them his. He wrote desperate messages and pressed them into their hands and said Alice Springs. Alice Springs. Alice Springs. Over and over until it meant nothing. *Alicesprings. Alispringsalisbrings*. The words and the paper slipped through their fingers as if they were sand.

Lasseter believes it was the kaditcha man who had it in for him the whole time. He looks out towards the mulga tree again. And in the blackness he can see it moving. Dancing. It has become the kaditcha man again. He has resumed his human form. He is dancing. Lasseter can hear the soft pad pad of his feet on the sand. As soft as the whisper of paranoia. He can make out the white markings on his skin. Sees the movement. He knows he is dancing him. Singing him.

'Fuck him!' says Lasseter. 'If I had another bullet left he wouldn't be so game.'

He looks around for his gun. It's gone. He forgot for a moment. He lost it years ago. He closes his eyes and tries to remember the first feeling of finding the gold once more. The exhilaration of it. Standing in the middle of a wilderness, untrodden by white men. Nuggets all around him. As thick as plums in a pudding. Pure like the golden tablets of the archangel. He was standing on one of the largest reefs of gold in the world. His reef. His empire! The gold fever made his whole body shake.

That was when he still had his gun. Before his camels ran away. Before the blacks encircled him. Held a council and decided to feed him. Listened to his words of wealth and prosperity. He told them about his dream of great gold mines. Of herds of stock fed and watered by artesian bores. How he would develop the land. How it made him the richest man in the world. And they asked him why the richest man in the world was also a beggar.

Poor beggar me.

But the blacks didn't trust him. The land here was sacred to them. They didn't want him to dig it up. They even took out his claim pegs. They didn't understand the value of the land.

'Fuck 'em,' he says, they're all dead now.

He wakes with the sunrise. The sand blight is bad today. *Una pika purlka*, the blacks said looking at his eyes. The sun is blinding. But he can make out someone coming towards him. Walking slowly across the desert. He tenses. The warriors came down to him with two spears each. Ready to spear him to death. But they saw how close to death he was and left him. Left him to the elements and the songs of the kaditcha man. They didn't understand that he was the richest man in the world.

It is one of the tribal women coming towards him. He can see her now. She kneels on the ground in front of him and begins digging in the sand. Looking for yams maybe. He looks at her smooth dark skin. At her breasts. God he could do with a feed, he thinks. Maybe a steak. A real big one, like they used to cook at Alice Springs. Red juices running down his chin. Suddenly she is gone. Blended into the desert.

It's midday. The shadows are hiding. The sky above is so blue you could fall up into it and drown if you didn't hang onto the ground. He closes his eyes again. Shuts out the bright glare of the desert and sun. It's much clearer in the dark. And he can see the blacks out there dancing again. All their bodies marked white. Like the stars.

He clung on for days waiting for the rescue team. The expedition party. The aeroplane. They never came. He sat in the small alcove, up against the reef, waiting vainly for them. As his life ebbed slowly out of him. *Kuna kuna. Pika purlka.* They'd come in their own time. Looking for his bones. But they didn't realise that he had to be there when they arrived. They needed him to show them the gold. To show them it wasn't just rock.

He could feel the gold deep down there beneath him. A large vein of it that ran through the earth all the way from Kalgoorlie. A whole river of gold. As vast as the Milky Way. And how many times had he sworn he would trade it all for the simplest thing — a bite of bread, a swig of water, or even release?

And Lasseter wishes he could pray. He used to once. But he has gone his own way for so long that he feels he can't even summon the words any more.

It's late in the afternoon again now. The sun is setting. The shadows creep towards him again. The kaditcha's mulga fingers reach out to grab him once more. The black shadow crosses his thin leg. The shiver runs through him, shaking him like a fever.

Then it passes. It is that time again. That miraculous instant. The sharp brightness flares across the rock face. All along the side of the reef. It is gold. And he is gold too. He is the reef.

Then it fades. He feels the cold greyness of stone return to his limbs. He waits for the stars as the sky turns black. And he can see the people of the tribe dancing out there. Renewing the land. Reinvigorating themselves. Thousands of them. Ten of thousands of them.

Ridgestmanninawurl! Ridgestmanninawurl!

He once thought they didn't understand. Didn't know the value of the land. But that was before they all went up to the stars. They knew all right. That's why they left him there. Anchored to the gold. Dragging him into the rock face. Unable to ever rise up to the heavens.

Bibliography

Terra Nullius — the Unknown Country

Rienits, R and T, *The Voyages of Captain Cook*, Paul Hamlyn, Sydney, NSW, 1968.

Wharton, Captain WJL, *Captain Cook's Journal during His First Voyage Round the World Made in H.M. Bark Endeavour, 1768–71*, Elliot Stock, London, UK, 1893.

Buckley's Chance

Hill, B, *Ghosting William Buckley*, William Heinemann Australia, Melbourne, Vic, 1993.

Morgan, J, *The Life and Adventures of William Buckley*, Archibald MacDougall, Hobart, Tas, 1852.

Robertson, C, *Buckley's Hope*, Scribe Publications, Melbourne, Vic, 1980.

Wannan, B, *Australian Folklore*, Lansdowne, Melbourne, Vic, 1970.

Charles Darwin Views the Future

Darwin, C, *The Voyage of the Beagle*, Marshall Cavendish, London, UK, 1987.

Desmond, A and Moore, J, *Darwin*, Michael Joseph, London, UK, 1991.

Karp, W, *Charles Darwin and the Origin of the Species*, Cassell, London, UK, 1968.

The Last History of Jorgen Jorgensen

Clune, F, *The Viking of Van Diemens Land*, Angus and Robertson, Sydney, NSW, 1954.

Jorgensen, J, A Fragment of an Autobiography, in *The Hobart Town Almanac and Van Diemen's Land Annual*, part 1, James Ross, Hobart, 1835–36.

Plomley, NJB, *Jorgen Jorgensen and the Aborigines of Van Diemen's Land*, Blubber Head Press, Hobart, Tas, 1991.

Hogan, JF, *The Convict King*, J Walch and Sons, Hobart, Tas, 1891.

Sorry Business

Plomley, NJB, *Weep in Silence*, Blubber Head Press, Hobart, Tas, 1987.

Pybus, C, *Community of Thieves*, William Heinemann, Melbourne, Vic, 1991.

Rae-Ellis, V, *Black Robinson: Protector of Aborigines*, Melbourne University Press, Melbourne, Vic, 1988.

Roberts, Jan, *Jack of Cape Grimm*, Greenhouse Publications, Richmond, Vic, 1986.

The Unknown South Land

Drake-Brockman, H, *Voyage to Disaster*, Angus and Robertson, Sydney, NSW, 1963.

Harris, J, *One Blood*, Albatross Books, Sydney, NSW, 1989.

Holy Bible, King James version.

Stormon, EJ (ed), *The Salvado Memoirs*, University of Western Australia Press, Perth, WA, 1978.

The Story of New Norcia, The Benedictine Community of New Norcia, New Norcia, WA, 1991.

Do You Remember When You Heard Kennedy Had Been Killed?

Wannan, B, *Australian Folklore*, Lansdowne, Melbourne, Vic, 1970.

William Carron's Narrative of Kennedy's Cape York Expedition, Corkwood Press, Bundaberg, Qld, 1996.

Illustrated History of Australia, Paul Hamlyn, Sydney, NSW, 1974.

The Three Gospels of the Reverend Lancelot Threlkeld

Harris, J, *One Blood: 200 Years of Aboriginal Encounter with Christianity*, Albatross Books, Sydney, NSW, 1989.

Threlkeld, Reverend L, *An Australian Language As Spoken by the Awabakal, the people of Awaba or Lake Maquarie, Being an Account of Their Language, Traditions and Customs* (J Fraser, ed), Government Printer, Sydney, NSW, 1892.

Threlkeld, Reverend L, *A Statement Chiefly Relating to the Formation and Abandonment of a Mission to the Aborigines of New South Wales*, Government Printer, Sydney, NSW, 1828.

Dig: The Forgotten History of Burke and Wills

Clark, CMH, *A History of Australia*, vol IV, Melbourne University Press, Melbourne, Vic, 1978.

Clune, F, *Dig: The Burke and Wills Saga*, Angus and Robertson, Sydney, NSW, 1937.

Bonyhady, T, *Burke and Wills: From Melbourne to Myth*, David Ell Press, Sydney, NSW, 1991.

The Event of the Century

Arnold, P, and Wynne-Thomas, P, *The Ashes: A Complete Illustrated History*, Brian Trodd Publishing House Ltd, London, UK, 1990.

Moyes, AG 'Johnnie', *Australian Cricket — a History*, Angus and Robertson, Sydney, NSW, 1959.

Mulvaney, DJ, *Cricket Walkabout*, Melbourne University Press, Melbourne, Vic, 1967.

Mulvaney, DJ and Harcourt, R, *Cricket Walkabout*, Macmillan, Melbourne, Vic, 1988.

Wood, JG, *The Natural History of Man*, George Routledge and Sons, London, UK, 1870.

Illustrated History of Australia, Paul Hamlyn, Sydney, NSW, 1974.

Ned Kelly Dreaming

Clark, CMH, *A History of Australia*, vol iv, Melbourne University Press, Melbourne, Vic, 1978.

Jones, I, *Ned Kelly: A Short Life*, Lothian, Melbourne, Vic, 1994.

Mrs Watson Escapes the Cannibals

Robertson, J, *Lizard Island: A Reconstruction of the Life of Mrs Watson of Lizard Island*, Hutchinson, Melbourne, Vic, 1981.

The Heroine of Lizard Island, Cooktown Shire Council, Cooktown, Qld, 1956.

Wannan, B, *Australian Folklore*, Lansdowne, Melbourne, Vic, 1970.

Krao — the Missing Link

Stolen Lives exhibition, curated by Roslyn Poignant, National Library of Australia, Canberra, ACT, 1997.

Jandamarrajandamarrajandamarra!

Idriess, I, *Outlaws of the Leopolds*, Angus and Robertson, Sydney, NSW, 1952.

Nicholson, J, *Kimberley Warrior*, Allen and Unwin, Sydney, NSW, 1997.

Pedersen, H and Worramorra, B, *Jandamarra and the Binuba Resistance*, Magabala Books, Broome, WA, 1994.

The Last Battle

Dennison, D, *Mutiny on the Western Front*, Mingara Films, Sydney, NSW, 1979 (film).

Grasby, A and Hill, M, *Six Australian Battlefields*, Angus and Robertson, Sydney, NSW, 1988.

History of the 20th Century, vol 2, BPC Publishing, London, UK, 1968.

Mrs Shackleton's Freezer

Hurley, F, *Shackleton's Argonauts: The Epic Tale of Shackleton's Voyage to Antarctica in 1918*, McGraw Hill, Sydney, NSW, 1979.

Shackleton, EH, *South: The Story of Shackleton's Last Expedition, 1914–1917*, Century, London, UK, 1983.

Antarctica, Reader's Digest Books, Sydney, NSW, 1985.

Pastor Strehlow's Journey to the Land of Death

Harris, J, *One Blood: 200 Years of Aboriginal Encounter with Christianity*, Albatross Books, Sydney, NSW, 1989.

Strehlow, TGH, *Journey to Horse Shoe Bend*, Angus and Robertson, Sydney, NSW, 1969.

Strehlow, TGH, *Songs of Central Australia*, Angus and Robertson, Sydney, NSW, 1971.

Lasseter's Last Dream

Idriess, I, *Lasseter's Last Ride*, Angus and Robertson, Sydney, NSW, 1931.

Stoneking, BM, *Lasseter — the Making of a Legend*, Allen and Unwin, Sydney, NSW, 1985.